"He's dying," I said. "There's nothing I can do for him. It's just a matter of time."

The landlady nodded.

"How old is he?" I asked.

"I heard you," the old man said from across the room. "You want to know how old I am."

"How old are you?"

"I'm one year old."

RICHARD MATHESON

SHOCK II

A BERKLEY BOOK
published by
BERKLEY PUBLISHING CORPORATION

ACKNOWLEDGMENTS

A FLOURISH OF STRUMPETS was originally published in *Playboy*. Copyright © 1956 by HMH Publishing Company, Inc.

BROTHER TO THE MACHINE was originally published in *IF*. Copyright 1952 by Quinn Publishing Co., Inc.

NO SUCH THING AS A VAMPIRE was originally published in *Playboy*. Copyright © 1959 by HMH Publishing Co., Inc.

DESCENT was originally published in *IF*. Copyright 1954 by Quinn Publishing Co., Inc.

DEADLINE was originally published in *Rogue*. Copyright © 1959 by Richard Matheson.

THE MAN WHO MADE THE WORLD was originally published in *Imagination*. Copyright 1953 by Greenleaf Publishing Co.

GRAVEYARD SHIFT was originally published in *Ed McBain's Mystery Book* as THE FACES. Copyright © 1960 by Pocket Books, Inc.

THE LIKENESS OF JULIE, by "Logan Swanson" was originally published in ALONE BY NIGHT, Ballantine Books, New York. Copyright © 1962, by Richard Matheson.

LAZARUS II was originally published in *Fantastic Story Magazine*. Copyright © 1953 by Best Books, Inc.

BIG SURPRISE was originally published in *Ellery Queen's Mystery Magazine* as WHAT WAS IN THE BOX. Copyright © 1959 by Davis Publishing Co.

CRICKETS was originally published in *Shock Magazine*. Copyright © 1960 by Richard Matheson

MUTE was originally published in THE FIEND IN YOU, Ballantine Books, New York. Copyright © 1962 by Richard Matheson.

FROM SHADOWED PLACES was originally published in *Fantasy and Science Fiction*. Copyright © 1960 by Mercury Press, Inc.

Contents

SHOCK II

A Flourish of Strumpets

ONE EVENING IN 1959 the doorbell rang.

Frank and Sylvia Gussett had just settled down to watch television. Frank put his gin and tonic on the table and stood. He walked into the hall and opened the door.

It was a woman.

"Good evening," she said. "I represent the Exchange."

"The exchange?" Frank smiled politely.

"Yes," said the woman. "We're beginning an experimental program in this neighborhood. As to our service—"

Their service was a venerable one. Frank gaped.

"Are you *serious?*" he asked.

"Perfectly," the woman said.

"But—good Lord, you can't—come to our very houses and—and—that's against the law! I can have you arrested!"

"Oh, you wouldn't want to do *that,*" said the woman. She absorbed blouse-enhancing air.

"Oh, wouldn't I?" said Frank and closed the door in her face.

He stood there breathing hard. Outside, he heard the sound of the woman's spike heels clacking down the porch steps and fading off.

Frank stumbled into the living room.

"Its unbelievable," he said.

Sylvia looked up from the television set. "What is?" she asked.

He told her.

"What!" She rose from her chair, aghast.

They stood looking at each other a moment. Then Sylvia strode to the phone and picked up the receiver. She spun the dial and told the operator, *"I want the police."*

"Strange business," said the policeman who arrived a few minutes later.

"Strange indeed," mused Frank.

"Well, what are you going to *do* about it?" challenged Sylvia.

"Not much we *can* do right off, ma'am," explained the policeman. "Nothing to go on."

"But my description—" said Frank.

"We can't go around arresting every woman we see in spike heels and a white blouse," said the policeman. "If she comes back, you let us know. Probably just a sorority prank, though."

"Perhaps he's right," said Frank when the patrol car had driven off.

Sylvia replied, "He'd better be."

"Strangest thing happened last night," said Frank to Maxwell as they drove to work.

Maxwell snickered. "Yeah, she came to our house too," he said.

"She did?" Frank glanced over, startled, at his grinning neighbor.

"Yeah," said Maxwell. "Just my luck the old lady had to answer the door."

Frank stiffened. *"We* called the police," he said.

"What for?" asked Maxwell. "Why fight it?"

Frank's brow furrowed. "You mean you—don't think it was a sorority girl prank?" he asked.

"Hell, no, man," said Maxwell, "it's for real." He began to sing:

I'm just a poor little
    door-to-door whore;
A want-to-be good
But misunderstood . . .

"What on earth?" asked Frank.

"Heard it at a stag party," said Maxwell. "Guess this isn't the first town they've hit."

"Good Lord," muttered Frank, blanching.

"Why not?" asked Maxwell. "It was just a matter of time. Why should they let all that home trade go to waste?"

"That's *execrable,"* declared Frank.

"Hell it is," said Maxwell. "It's progress."

The second one came that night; a black-root blonde, slit-skirted and sweatered to within an inch of her breathing life.

"Hel-lo, honey," she said when Frank opened the door. "The name's Janie. Interested?"

Frank stood rigid to the heels. "I—" he said.

"Twenty-three and fancy free," said Janie.

Frank shut the door, quivering.

"Again?" asked Sylvia as he tottered back.

"Yes," he mumbled.

"Did you get her address and phone number so we can tell the police?"

"I forgot," he said.

"Oh!" Sylvia stamped her mule. "You said you were going to."

"I know." Frank swallowed. "Her name was— Janie."

"That's a *big* help," Sylvia said. She shivered. *"Now* what are we going to do?"

Frank shook his head.

"Oh, this is *monstrous,"* she said. "That we should be

exposed to such—" She trembled with fury.

Frank embraced her. "Courage," he whispered.

"I'll get a dog," she said. "A vicious one."

"No, no," he said, "we'll call the police again. They'll simply have to station someone out here."

Sylvia began to cry. "It's monstrous," she sobbed, "that's all."

"Monstrous," he agreed.

"What's that you're humming?" she asked at breakfast.

He almost spewed out whole wheat toast.

"Nothing," he said, choking. "Just a song I heard."

She patted him on the back. "Oh."

He left the house, mildly shaken. It *is* monstrous, he thought.

That morning, Sylvia bought a sign at a hardware store and hammered it into the front lawn. It read NO SOLICITING. She underlined the SOLICITING. Later she went out again and underlined the underline.

"Came right to your door you say?" asked the FBI man Frank phoned from the office.

"Right to the door," repeated Frank, "bold as you please."

"My, my," said the FBI man. He clucked.

"Notwithstanding," said Frank sternly, "the police have refused to station a man in our neighborhood."

"I see," said the FBI man.

"Something has got to be done," declared Frank. "This is a gross invasion of privacy."

"It certainly is," said the FBI man, "and we will look into the matter, never fear."

After Frank had hung up, the FBI man returned to his bacon sandwich and thermos of buttermilk.

"I'm just a poor little—" he had sung before catching himself. Shocked, he totted figures the remainder of his lunch hour.

● ● ●

The next night it was a perky brunette with a blouse front slashed to forever.

"No!" said Frank in a ringing voice.

She wiggled sumptuously. "Why?" she asked.

"I do not have to explain myself to you!" he said and shut the door, heart pistoning against his chest.

Then he snapped his fingers and opened the door again. The brunette turned, smiling.

"Changed your mind, honey?" she asked.

"No. I mean *yes,*" said Frank, eyes narrowing. "What's your address?"

The brunette looked mildly accusing.

"Now, honey," she said. "You wouldn't be trying to get me in trouble, would you?"

"She wouldn't tell me," he said dismally when he returned to the living room.

Sylvia looked despairing. "I phoned the police again," she said.

"And—?"

"And *nothing*. There's the smell of corruption in this."

Frank nodded gravely. "You'd better get that dog," he said. He thought of the brunette. "A *big* one," he added.

"Wowee, that Janie," said Maxwell.

Frank down shifted vigorously and yawed around a corner on squealing tires. His face was adamantine.

Maxwell clapped him on the shoulder.

"Aw, come off it, Frankie-boy," he said, "you're not fooling me any. You're no different from the rest of us."

"I'll have no part in it," declared Frank, "and that's all there is to it."

"So keep telling that to the Mrs.," said Maxwell. "But get in a few kicks on the side like the rest of us. Right?"

"Wrong," said Frank. *"All* wrong. No *wonder* the

police can't do anything. I'm probably the only willing witness in town."

Maxwell guffawed.

It was a raven-haired, limp-lidded vamp that night. On her outfit spangles moved and glittered at strategic points.

"Hel-*lo*, honey lamb," she said. "My name's—"

"*What have you done with our dog?*" challenged Frank.

"Why, nothing, honey, nothing," she said. "He's just off getting acquainted with my poodle Winifred. Now about *us*—"

Frank shut the door without a word and waited until the twitching had eased before returning to Sylvia and television.

Semper, by God oh God, he thought as he put on his pajamas later, *fidelis.*

The next two nights they sat in the darkened living room and, as soon as the women rang the doorbell, Sylvia phoned the police.

"*Yes,*" she whispered, furiously, "they're right out there *now*. Will you please send a patrol car *this instant?*"

Both nights the patrol car arrived after the women had gone.

"Complicity," muttered Sylvia as she daubed on cold cream. "Plain out-and-out complicity."

Frank ran cold water over his wrists.

That day Frank phoned city and state officials who promised to look into the matter.

That night it was a redhead sheathed in a green knit dress that hugged all that was voluminous and there was much of that.

"Now, see here—" Frank began.

"Girls who were here before me," said the redhead, "tell me you're not interested. Well, I always say, where there's a disinterested husband there's a listening wife."

"Now you see here—" said Frank.

He stopped as the redhead handed him a card. He looked at it automatically.

39-26-36

MARGIE
(specialties)

By appointment only

"If you don't want to set it up here, honey," said Margie, "you just meet me in the Cyprian Room of the Hotel Fillmore."

"I *beg* your pardon," said Frank and flung the card away.

"Any evening between six and seven," Margie chirped.

Frank leaned against the shut door and birds with heated wings buffeted at his face.

"Monstrous," he said with a gulp. "Oh, m-*monstrous.*"

"*Again?*" asked Sylvia.

"But with a difference," he said vengefully. "I have traced them to their lair and tomorrow I shall lead the police there."

"Oh, Frank!" said Sylvia, embracing him. "You're wonderful."

"Th-thank you," said Frank.

When he came out of the house the next morning he found the card on one of the porch steps. He picked it up and slid it into his wallet.

Sylvia mustn't see it, he thought.

It would hurt her.

Besides he had to keep the porch neat.

Besides, it was important evidence.

That evening he sat in a shadowy Cyprian Room booth revolving a glass of sherry between two fingers.

Jukebox music softly thrummed; there was the mumble of post-work conversation in the air.

Now, thought Frank. *When Margie arrives, I'll duck into the phone booth and call the police, then keep her occupied in conversation until they come. That's what I'll do. When Margie—*

Margie arrived.

Frank sat like a Medusa victim. Only his mouth moved. It opened slowly. His gaze rooted on the jutting opulence of Margie as she waggled along the aisle, then came to gelatinous rest on a leather-topped bar stool.

Five minutes later he cringed out a side door.

"Wasn't *there?*" asked Sylvia for a third time.

"I *told* you," snapped Frank, concentrating on his breaded cutlet.

Sylvia was still a moment. Then her fork clinked down.

"We'll have to move, then," she said. "Obviously, the authorities have no intention of doing *anything.*"

"What difference does it make *where* we live?" he mumbled.

She didn't reply.

"I mean," he said, trying to break the painful silence, "well, who knows, maybe it's an inevitable cultural phenomenon. Maybe—"

"*Frank Gussett!*" she cried. "*Are you defending that awful Exchange?*"

"No, no, of course not," he blurted. "It's execrable. Really! But—well, maybe it's Greece all over again. Maybe it's Rome. Maybe it's—"

"I don't care *what* it is!" she cried. "It's *awful!*"

He put his hand on hers. "There, there," he said. *39-26-36,* he thought.

That night, in the frantic dark, there was a desperate reaffirmation of their love.

"It *was* nice, *wasn't* it?" asked Sylvia, plaintively.

"Of course," he said. *39-26-36.*

● ● ●

"That's right!" said Maxwell as they drove to work the next morning, "a cultural phenomenon. You hit it on the head, Frankie boy. An inevitable goddamn cultural phenomenon. First the houses. Then the lady cab drivers, the girls on street corners, the clubs, the teen-age pickups roaming the drive-in movies. Sooner or later they had to branch out more; put it on a door-to-door basis. And naturally, the syndicates are going to run it, pay off complainers. Inevitable. You're so right, Frankie boy; so right."

Frank drove on, nodding grimly.

Over lunch he found himself humming, *"Mar-gie. I'm always thinkin' of you—"*

He stopped, shaken. He couldn't finish the meal. He prowled the streets until one, marble-eyed. The mass mind, he thought, that evil old mass mind.

Before he went into his office he tore the little card to confetti and snowed it into a disposal can.

In the figures he wrote that afternoon the number 39 cropped up with dismaying regularity.

Once with an exclamation point.

"I almost think you *are* defending this—this *thing*," accused Sylvia. "You and your cultural phenomenons!"

Frank sat in the living room listening to her bang dishes in the kitchen sink. Cranky old thing, he thought.

MARGIE
(specialties)

Will you stop! he whispered furiously to his mind.

That night while he was brushing his teeth, he started to sing, *"I'm just a poor little—"*

"Damn!" he muttered to his wide-eyed reflection.

That night there were dreams. Unusual ones.

The next day he and Sylvia argued.

The next day Maxwell told him his system.

The next day Frank muttered to himself more than once, "I'm so tired of it all."

The next night the women stopped coming.

"Is it *possible?*" said Sylvia. "Are they actually going to leave us alone?"

Frank held her close. "Looks like it," he said faintly. *Oh, I'm despicable,* he thought.

A week went by. No women came. Frank woke daily at six A.M. and did a little dusting and vacuuming before he left for work.

"I like to help you," he said when Sylvia asked. She looked at him strangely. When he brought home bouquets three nights in a row she put them in water with a quizzical look on her face.

It was the following Wednesday night.

The doorbell rang. Frank stiffened. They'd *promised* to stop coming!

"I'll get it," he said.

"Do," she said.

He clumped to the door and opened it.

"Evening, sir."

Frank stared at the handsome, mustached young man in the jaunty sports clothes.

"I'm from the Exchange," the man said. "Wife home?"

Brother to the Machine

HE STEPPED INTO the sunlight and walked among the people. His feet carried him away from the black tube depths. The distant roar of underground machinery left his brain to be replaced by myriad whispers of the city.

Now he was walking the main street. Men of flesh and men of steel passed him by, coming and going. His legs moved slowly and his footsteps were lost in a thousand footsteps.

He passed a building that had died in the last war. There were scurrying men and robots pulling off the rubble to build again. Over their heads hung the control ship and he saw men looking down to see that work was done properly.

He slipped in and out among the crowd. No fear of being seen. Only inside of him was there a difference. Eyes would never know it. Visio-poles set at every corner could not glean the change. In form and visage he was just like all the rest.

He looked at the sky. He was the only one. The others didn't know about the sky. It was only when you broke away that you could see. He saw a rocket ship flashing across the sun and control ships hovering in a sky rich with blue and fluffy clouds.

The dull-eyed people glanced at him suspiciously and hurried on. The blank-faced robots made no sign. They clanked on past, holding their envelopes and their packages in long metal arms.

He lowered his eyes and kept walking. A man cannot look at the sky, he thought. It is suspect to look at the sky.

"Would you help a buddy?"

He paused and his eyes flicked down to the card on the man's chest.

Ex-Space Pilot. Blind. Legalized Beggar.

Signed by the stamp of the Control Commissioner. He put his hand on the blind man's shoulder. The man did not speak but passed by and moved on, his cane clacking on the sidewalk until he had disappeared. It was not allowed to beg in this district. They would find him soon.

He turned from watching and strode on. The visiopoles had seen him pause and touch the blind man. It was not permitted to pause on business streets, to touch another.

He passed a metal news dispenser and, brushing by, pulled out a sheet. He continued on and held it up before his eyes.

Income Taxes Raised. Military Draft Raised. Prices Raised.

Those were the story heads. He turned it over. On the back was an editorial that told why Earth forces had been compelled to destroy all the Martians.

Something clicked in his mind and his fingers closed slowly into a tight fist.

He passed his people, men and robots both. What distinction now? he asked himself. The common classes did the same work as the robots. Together they walked or drove through the streets carrying and delivering.

To be a man, he thought. No longer is it a blessing, a pride, a gift. To be brother to the machine, used and broken by invisible men who kept their eyes on poles and their fists bunched in ships that hung over all their heads, waiting to strike at opposition.

When it came to you one day that this was so, you saw there was no reason to go on with it.

He stopped in the shade and his eyes blinked. He looked in the shop window. There were tiny baby creatures in a cage.

Buy a Venus Baby For Your Child, said the card.

He looked into the eyes of the small tentacled things and saw there intelligence and pleading misery. And he passed on, ashamed of what one people can do to another people.

Something stirred within his body. He lurched a little and pressed his hand against his head. His shoulders twitched. When a man is sick, he thought, he cannot work. And when a man cannot work, he is not wanted.

He stepped into the street and a huge Control truck ground to a stop inches before him.

He walked away jerkily, leaped upon the sidewalk. Someone shouted and he ran. Now the photo-cells would follow him. He tried to lose himself in the moving crowds. People whirled by, an endless blur of faces and bodies.

They would be searching now. When a man stepped in front of a vehicle he was suspect. To wish death was not allowed. He had to escape before they caught him and took him to the Adjustment Center. He couldn't bear that.

People and robots rushed past him, messengers, delivery boys, the bottom level of an era. All going somewhere. In all these scurrying thousands, only he had no place to go, no bundle to deliver, no slavish duty to perform. He was adrift.

Street after street, block on block. He felt his body weaving. He was going to collapse soon, he felt. He was weak. He wanted to stop. But he couldn't stop. Not now. If he paused—sat down to rest—they would come for him and take him to the Adjustment Center. He didn't want to be adjusted. He didn't want to be made once more into a stupid shuffling machine. It was better to be in anguish and to understand.

He stumbled on. Bleating horns tore at his brain. Neon eyes blinked down at him as he walked.

He tried to walk straight but his system was giving way. Were they following? He would have to be careful. He kept his face blank and he walked as steadily as he could.

His knee joint stiffened and, as he bent to rub it in his hands, a wave of darkness leaped from the ground and clawed at him. He staggered against a plate glass window.

He shook his head and saw a man staring from inside. He pushed away. The man came out and stared at him in fear. The photo-cells picked him up and followed him. He had to hurry. He couldn't be brought back to start all over again. He'd rather be dead.

A sudden idea. Cold water. Only to drink?

I'm going to die, he thought. But I will know why I am dying and that will be different. I have left the laboratory where, daily, I was sated with calculations for bombs and gases and bacterial sprays.

All through those long days and nights of plotting destruction, the truth was growing in my brain. Connections were weakening, indoctrinations faltering as effort fought with apathy.

And, finally, something gave, and all that was left was weariness and truth and a great desire to be at peace.

And now he had escaped and he would never go back. His brain had snapped forever and they would never adjust him again.

He came to the citizen's park, last outpost for the old, the crippled, the useless. Where they could hide away and rest and wait for death.

He entered through the wide gate and looked at the high walls which stretched beyond eye. The walls that hid the ugliness from outside eyes. It was safe here. They did not care if a man died inside the citizen's park.

This is my island, he thought. I have found a silent place. There are no probing photo-cells here and no ears listening. A person can be free here.

His legs felt suddenly weak and he leaned against a blackened dead tree and sank down into the mouldy leaves lying deep on the ground.

An old man came by and stared at him suspiciously. The old man walked on. He could not stop to talk for minds were still the same even when the shackles had been burst.

Two old ladies passed him by. They looked at him and whispered to one another. He was not an old person. He was not allowed in the citizen's park. The Control Police might follow him. There was danger and they hurried on, casting frightened glances over their lean shoulders. When he came near they scurried over the hill.

He walked. Far off he heard a siren. The high, screeching siren of the Control Police cars. Were they after him? Did they know he was there? He hurried on, his body twitching as he loped up a sunbaked hill and down the other side. The lake, he thought, I am looking for the lake.

He saw a fountain and stepped down the slope and stood by it. There was an old man bent over it. It was the man who had passed him. The old man's lips enveloped the thin stream of water.

He stood there quietly, shaking. The old man did not know he was there. He drank and drank. The water dashed and sparkled in the sun. His hands reached out for the old man. The old man felt his touch and jerked away, water running across his gray bearded chin. He backed away, staring open-mouthed. He turned quickly and hobbled away.

He saw the old man run. Then he bent over the fountain. The water gurgled into his mouth. It ran down and up into his mouth and poured out again, tastelessly.

He straightened up suddenly, a sick burning in his chest. The sun faded to his eye, the sky became black. He stumbled about on the pavement, his mouth opening and closing. He tripped over the edge of the walk and fell to his knees on the dry ground.

He crawled in on the dead grass and fell on his back, his stomach grinding, water running over his chin.

He lay there with the sun shining on his face and he looked at it without blinking. Then he raised his hands and put them over his eyes.

An ant crawled across his wrist. He looked at it stupidly. Then he put the ant between two fingers and squashed it to a pulp.

He sat up. He couldn't stay where he was. Already they might be searching the park, their cold eyes scanning the hills, moving like a horrible tide through this last outpost where old people were allowed to think if they were able to.

He got up and staggered around clumsily and started up the path, stiff-legged, looking for the lake.

He turned a bend and walked in a weaving line. He heard whistles. He heard a distant shout. They *were* looking for him. Even here in the citizen's park where he thought he could escape. And find the lake in peace.

He passed an old shut down merry-go-round. He saw the little wooden horses in gay poses, galloping high and motionless, caught fast in time. Green and orange with heavy tassels, all thick covered with dust.

He reached a sunken walk and started down it. There were gray stone walls on both sides. Sirens were all around in the air. They knew he was loose and they were coming to get him now. A man could not escape. It was not done.

He shuffled across the road and moved up the path. Turning, he saw, far off, men running. They wore black uniforms and they were waving at him. He hurried on, his feet thudding endlessly on the concrete walk.

He ran off the path and up a hill and tumbled in the grass. He crawled into scarlet-leaved bushes and watched through waves of dizziness as the men of the Control Police dashed by.

Then he got up and started off, limping, his eyes staring ahead.

At last. The shifting, dull glitter of the lake. He hurried on now, stumbling and tripping. Only a little way. He lurched across a field. The air was thick with the smell of rotting grass. He crashed through the bushes and there were shouts and someone fired a gun. He looked back stiffly to see the men running after him.

He plunged into the water, flopping on his chest with a great splash. He struggled forward, walking on the bottom until the water had flooded over his chest, his shoulders, his head. Still walking while it washed into his mouth and filled his throat and weighted his body, dragging him down.

His eyes were wide and staring as he slid gently forward onto his face on the bottom. His fingers closed in the silt and he made no move.

Later, the Control Police dragged him out and threw him in the black truck and drove off.

And, inside, the technician tore off the sheeting and shook his head at the sight of tangled coils and water-soaked machinery.

"They go bad," he muttered as he probed with pliers and picks. "They crack up and think they are men and go wandering. Too bad they don't work as good as people."

No Such Thing as a Vampire

IN THE EARLY autumn of the year 18—Madame Alexis Gheria awoke one morning to a sense of utmost torpor. For more than a minute, she lay inertly on her back, her dark eyes staring upward. How wasted she felt. It seemed as if her limbs were sheathed in lead. Perhaps she was ill. Petre must examine her and see.

Drawing in a faint breath, she pressed up slowly on an elbow. As she did, her nightdress slid, rustling, to her waist. How had it come unfastened? she wondered, looking down at herself.

Quite suddenly, Madame Gheria began to scream.

In the breakfast room, Dr. Petre Gheria looked up, startled, from his morning paper. In an instant, he had pushed his chair back, slung his napkin on the table and was rushing for the hallway. He dashed across its carpeted breadth and mounted the staircase two steps at a time.

It was a near hysterical Madame Gheria he found sitting on the edge of her bed looking down in horror at her breasts. Across the dilated whiteness of them, a smear of blood lay drying.

Dr. Gheria dismissed the upstairs maid who stood frozen in the open doorway, gaping at her mistress. He locked the door and hurried to his wife.

"Petre!" she gasped.

"Gently." He helped her lie back across the bloodstained pillow.

22

"Petre, what *is* it?" she begged.

"Lie still, my dear." His practiced hands moved in swift search over her breasts. Suddenly, his breath choked off. Pressing aside her head, he stared down dumbly at the pinprick lancinations on her neck, the ribbon of tacky blood that twisted downward from them.

"My *throat*," Alexis said.

"No, it's just a—" Dr. Gheria did not complete the sentence. He knew exactly what it was.

Madame Gheria began to tremble. "Oh, my God, my *God*," she said.

Dr. Gheria rose and foundered to the wash basin. Pouring in water, he returned to his wife and washed away the blood. The wound was clearly visible now— two tiny punctures close to the jugular. A grimacing Dr. Gheria touched the mounds of inflamed tissue in which they lay. As he did, his wife groaned terribly and turned her face away.

"Now listen to me," he said, his voice apparently calm. "We will not succumb, immediately, to superstition, do you hear? There are any number of—"

"I'm going to die," she said.

"Alexis, do you hear me?" He caught her harshly by the shoulders.

She turned her head and stared at him with vacant eyes. "You know what it is," she said.

Dr. Gheria swallowed. He could still taste coffee in his mouth.

"I know what it appears to be," he said, "and we shall—not ignore the possibility. However—"

"I'm going to die," she said.

"Alexis!" Dr. Gheria took her hand and gripped it fiercely. *"You shall not be taken from me,"* he said.

Solta was a village of some thousand inhabitants situated in the foothills of Rumania's Bihor Mountains. It was a place of dark traditions. People, hearing the bay of distant wolves, would cross themselves without a thought. Children would gather garlic buds as other children gather flowers, bringing them home for the windows. On every door there was a painted cross, at every throat a metal one. Dread of the vampire's blighting was as normal as the dread of fatal sickness. It was always in the air.

Dr. Gheria thought about that as he bolted shut the windows of Alexis' room. Far off, molten twilight hung above the mountains. Soon it would be dark again. Soon the citizens of Solta would be barricaded in their garlic-reeking houses. He had no doubt that every soul of them knew exactly what had happened to his wife. Already the cook and upstairs maid were pleading for discharge. Only the inflexible discipline of the butler, Karel, kept them at their jobs. Soon, even that would not suffice. Before the horror of the vampire, reason fled.

He'd seen the evidence of it that very morning when he'd ordered Madame's room stripped to the walls and searched for rodents or venomous insects. The servants had moved about the room as if on a floor of eggs, their eyes more white than pupil, their fingers twitching constantly to their crosses. They had known full well no rodents or insects would be found. And Gheria had known it. Still, he'd raged at them for their timidity, succeeding only in frightening them further.

He turned from the window with a smile.

"There now," he said, "nothing alive will enter this room tonight."

He caught himself immediately, seeing the flare of terror in her eyes.

"Nothing at *all* will enter," he amended.

Alexis lay motionless on her bed, one pale hand at her breast, clutching at the worn silver cross she'd taken from her jewel box. She hadn't worn it since he'd given her the diamond-studded one when they were married. How typical of her village background that, in this moment of dread, she should seek protection from the unadorned cross of her church. She was such a child. Gheria smiled down gently at her.

"You won't be needing that, my dear," he said, "you'll be safe tonight."

Her fingers tightened on the crucifix.

"No, no, wear it if you will," he said. "I only meant that I'll be at your side all night."

"You'll stay with me?"

He sat on the bed and held her hand.

"Do you think I'd leave you for a moment?" he said.

Thirty minutes later, she was sleeping. Dr. Gheria drew a chair beside the bed and seated himself. Removing his glasses, he massaged the bridge of his nose with the thumb and forefinger of his left hand. Then, sighing, he began to watch his wife. How incredibly beautiful she was. Dr. Gheria's breath grew strained.

"There is no such thing as a vampire," he whispered to himself.

There was a distant pounding. Dr. Gheria muttered in his sleep, his fingers twitching. The pounding increased; an agitated voice came swirling from the darkness. "Doctor!" it called.

Gheria snapped awake. For a moment, he looked confusedly toward the locked door.

"Dr. Gheria?" demanded Karel.

"What?"

"Is everything all right?"

"Yes, everything is—"

Dr. Gheria cried out hoarsely, springing for the bed. Alexis' nightdress had been torn away again. A hideous dew of blood covered her chest and neck.

Karel shook his head.

"Bolted windows cannot hold away the creature, sir," he said.

He stood, tall and lean, beside the kitchen table on which lay the cluster of silver he'd been polishing when Gheria had entered.

"The creature has the power to make of itself a vapor which can pass through any opening however small," he said.

"But the cross!" cried Gheria. "It was still at her throat—untouched! Except by—blood," he added in a sickened voice.

"This I cannot understand," said Karel, grimly. "The cross should have protected her."

"But why did I see nothing?"

"You were drugged by its mephitic presence," Karel said. "Count yourself fortunate that you were not also attacked."

"I do not count myself fortunate!" Dr. Gheria struck his palm, a look of anguish on his face. "What am I to do, Karel?" he asked.

"Hang garlic," said the old man. "Hang it at the windows, at the doors. Let there be no opening unblocked by garlic."

Gheria nodded distractedly. "Never in my life have I seen this thing," he said, brokenly. "Now, my own wife—"

"I have seen it," said Karel. "I have, myself, put to its rest one of these monsters from the grave."

"The stake—?" Gheria looked revolted.

The old man nodded slowly.

Gheria swallowed. "Pray God you may put this one to rest as well," he said.

"Petre?"

She was weaker now, her voice a toneless murmur. Gheria bent over her. "Yes, my dear," he said.

"It will come again tonight," she said.

"No." He shook his head determinedly. "It cannot come. The garlic will repel it."

"My cross didn't," she said, "you didn't."

"The garlic will," he said. "And see?" He pointed at the bedside table. "I've had black coffee brought for me. I won't sleep tonight."

She closed her eyes, a look of pain across her sallow features.

"I don't want to die," she said. "Please don't let me die, Petre."

"You won't," he said. "I promise you; the monster shall be destroyed."

Alexis shuddered feebly. "But if there is no way, Petre," she murmured.

"There is always a way," he answered.

Outside, the darkness, cold and heavy, pressed around the house. Dr. Gheria took his place beside the bed and began to wait. Within the hour, Alexis slipped into a heavy slumber. Gently, Dr. Gheria released her hand and poured himself a cup of steaming coffee. As he sipped it, hotly bitter, he looked around the room. Door locked, windows bolted, every opening sealed with garlic, the cross at Alexis' throat. He nodded slowly to himself. It will work, he thought. The monster would be thwarted.

He sat there, waiting, listening to his breath.

Dr. Gheria was at the door before the second knock.

"Michael!" He embraced the younger man. "Dear Michael. I was sure you'd come!"

Anxiously, he ushered Dr. Vares toward his study. Outside darkness was just falling.

"Where on earth are all the people of the village?" asked Vares. "I swear I didn't see a soul as I rode in."

"Huddling, terror-stricken, in their houses, Gheria said, "and all my servants with them save for one."

"Who is that?"

"My butler, Karel," Gheria answered. "He didn't answer the door because he's sleeping. Poor fellow, he is very old and has been doing the work of five." He gripped Vares' arm. "Dear Michael," he said, "you have no idea how glad I am to see you."

Vares looked at him worriedly. "I came as soon as I received your message," he said.

"And I appreciate it," Gheria said. "I know how long and hard a ride it is from Cluj."

"What's wrong?" asked Vares. "Your letter only said—"

Quickly, Gheria told him what had happened in the past week.

I tell you, Michael, I stumble at the brink of madness," he said. "Nothing works! Garlic, wolfsbane, crosses, mirrors, running water—useless! No, don't say it! This isn't superstition nor imagination! This is *happening!* A vampire is destroying her! Each day she sinks yet deeper into that—deadly torpor from which—"

Gheria clenched his hands. "And yet I cannot understand it," he muttered, brokenly, "I simply cannot understand it."

"Come, sit, sit." Doctor Vares pressed the older man into a chair, grimacing at the pallor of him. Nervously, his fingers sought for Gheria's pulse beat.

"Never mind me," protested Gheria. "It's Alexis we must help." He pressed a sudden, trembling hand across his eyes. "Yet how?" he said.

He made no resistance as the younger man undid his collar and examined his neck.

"You, too," said Vares, sickened.

"What does that matter?" Gheria clutched at the younger man's hand. "My friend, my dearest friend," he said, "tell me that it is not I! Do *I* do this hideous thing to her?"

Vares looked confounded. *"You?"* he said. "But—"

"I know, I know," said Gheria, "I, myself, have been attacked. Yet nothing follows, Michael! What breed of horror is this which cannot be impeded? From what unholy place does it emerge? I've had the countryside examined foot by foot, every graveyard ransacked, every crypt inspected! There is no house within the village that has not been subjected to my search. I tell you, Michael, there is nothing! Yet, there is something—something which assaults us nightly, draining us of life. The village is engulfed by terror—and I as well! I never see this creature, never hear it! Yet, every morning, I find my beloved wife—"

Vares' face was drawn and pallid now. He stared intently at the older man.

"What am I to do, my friend?" pleaded Gheria. "How am I to save her?"

Vares had no answer.

"How long has she—been like this?" asked Vares. He could not remove his stricken gaze from the whiteness of Alexis' face.

"For days," said Gheria. "The retrogression has been constant."

Dr. Vares put down Alexis' flaccid hand. "Why did you not tell me sooner?" he asked.

"I thought the matter could be handled," Gheria answered, faintly. "I know now that it—cannot."

Vares shuddered. "But, surely—" he began.

"There is nothing left to be done," said Gheria. "Everything has been tried, *everything!*" He stumbled to the window and stared out bleakly into the deepening night. "And now it comes again," he murmured, "and we are helpless before it."

"Not helpless, Petro." Vares forced a cheering smile to his lips and laid his hand upon the older man's shoulder. "I will watch her tonight."

"It's useless."

"Not at all, my friend," said Vares, nervously. "And now you must sleep."

"I will not leave her," said Gheria.

"But you need rest."

"I cannot leave," said Gheria. "I will not be separated from her."

Vares nodded. "Of course," he said. "We will share the hours of watching then."

Gheria sighed. "We can try," he said, but there was no sound of hope in his voice.

Some 20 minutes later, he returned with an urn of steaming coffee which was barely possible to smell through the heavy mist of garlic fumes which hung in the air. Trudging to the bed, Gheria set down the tray. Dr. Vares had drawn a chair up beside the bed.

"I'll watch first," he said. "You sleep, Petre."

"It would do no good to try," said Gheria. He held a cup beneath the spigot and the coffee gurgled out like smoking ebony.

"Thank you," murmured Vares as the cup was handed to him. Gheria nodded once and drew himself a cupful before he sat.

"I do not know what will happen to Solta if this creature is not destroyed," he said. "The people are paralyzed by terror."

"Has it—been elsewhere in the village?" Vares asked him.

Gheria sighed exhaustedly. "Why need it go elsewhere?" he said. "It is finding all it—craves within these walls." He stared despondently at Alexis. "When we are gone," he said, "it will go elsewhere. The people know that and are waiting for it."

Vares set down his cup and rubbed his eyes.

"It seems impossible," he said, "that we, practitioners of a science, should be unable to—"

"What can science effect against it?" said Gheria. "Science which will not even admit its existence? We could bring, into this very room, the foremost scientists of the world and they would say—my friends, you have been deluded. There is no vampire. All is mere trickery."

Gheria stopped and looked intently at the younger man. He said, "Michael?"

Vares' breath was slow and heavy. Putting down his

cup of untouched coffee, Gheria stood and moved to where Vares sat slumped in his chair. He pressed back an eyelid, looked down briefly at the sightless pupil, then withdrew his hand. The drug was quick, he thought. And most effective. Vares would be insensible for more than time enough.

Moving to the closet, Gheria drew down his bag and carried it to the bed. He tore Alexis' nightdress from her upper body and, within seconds, had drawn another syringe full of her blood; this would be the last withdrawal, fortunately. Stanching the wound, he took the syringe to Vares and emptied it into the young man's mouth, smearing it across his lips and teeth.

That done, he strode to the door and unlocked it. Returning to Vares, he raised and carried him into the hall. Karel would not awaken; a small amount of opiate in his food had seen to that. Gheria labored down the steps beneath the weight of Vares' body. In the darkest corner of the cellar, a wooden casket waited for the younger man. There he would lie until the following morning when the distraught Dr. Petre Gheria would, with sudden inspiration, order Karel to search the attic and cellar on the remote, nay fantastic possibility that—

Ten minutes later, Gheria was back in the bedroom checking Alexis' pulse beat. It was active enough; she would survive. The pain and torturing horror she had undergone would be punishment enough for her. As for Vares—

Dr. Gheria smiled in pleasure for the first time since Alexis and he had returned from Cluj at the end of the summer. Dear spirits in heaven, would it not be sheer enchantment to watch old Karel drive a stake through Michael Vares' damned cuckolding heart!

Descent

It was impulse. Les pulled the car over to the curb and stopped it. He twisted the shiny key and the motor stopped. He turned to look across Sunset Boulevard, across the green hills that dropped away steeply to the ocean.

"Look, Ruth," he said.

It was late afternoon. Far out across the palisades they could see the Pacific shimmering with reflections of the red sun. The sky was a tapestry dripping gold and crimson. Streamers of billowy, pink-edged clouds hung across it.

"It's so pretty," Ruth said.

His hand lifted from the car seat to cover hers. She smiled at him a moment, then the smile faded as they watched the sunset again.

"It's hard to believe," Ruth said.

"What?" he asked.

"That we'll never see another."

He looked soberly at the brightly colored sky. Then he smiled but not in pleasure.

"Didn't we read that they'd have artificial sunsets?" he said. "You'll look out the windows of your room and see a sunset. Didn't we read that somewhere?"

"It won't be the same," she said, "Will it, Les?"

"How could it be?"

"I wonder," she murmured, "What it will really be like."

"A lot of people would like to know," he said.

They sat in silence watching the sun go down. It's funny, he thought, you try to get underneath to the real meaning of a moment like this but you can't. It passes and when it's over you don't know or feel any more than you did before. It's just one more moment added to the past. You *don't* appreciate what you have until it's taken away.

He looked over at Ruth and saw her looking solemnly and strangely at the ocean.

"Honey," he said quietly and gave her, with the word, his love.

She looked at him and tried to smile.

We'll still be together," he told her.

"I know," she said. "Don't pay any attention to me."

"But I will," he said, leaning over to kiss her cheek. "I'll look after you. Over the earth—"

"Or under it," she said.

Bill came out of the house to meet them. Les looked at his friend as he steered the car into the open concrete space by the garage. He wondered how Bill felt about leaving the house he'd just finished paying for. Free and clear, after eighteen years of payments, and tomorrow it would be rubble. Life is a bastard, he thought, switching off the engine.

"Hello, kid," Bill said to him. "Hi, beautiful," to Ruth.

"Hello handsome," Ruth said.

They got out of the car and Ruth took the package off the front seat. Bill's daughter Jeannie came running out of the house. "Hi, Les! Hi, Ruth!"

"Say, Bill, whose car are we going to take tomorrow?" Les asked him.

"I don't know, kid," Bill said. "We'll talk it over when Fred and Grace get here."

"Carry me piggy back Les," Jeannie demanded.

He swung her up. *I'm glad we don't have a child, I'd hate to take a child down there tomorrow.*

Mary looked up from the stove as they moved in.

They all said hello and Ruth put the package on the table.

"What's that?" Mary asked.

"I baked a pie," Ruth told her.

"Oh, you didn't have to do that," Mary said.

"Why not? It may be the last one I'll ever bake."

"It's not that bad," Bill said. "They'll have stoves down there."

"There'll be so much rationing it won't be worth the effort," Ruth said.

"The way my true love bakes that'll be good fortune," Bill said.

"Is *that* so!" Mary glared at her grinning husband, who patted her behind and moved into the living room with Les. Ruth stayed in the kitchen to help.

Les put down Bill's daughter.

Jeannie ran out. "Mama, I'm gonna help you make dinner!"

"How nice," they heard Mary say.

Les sank down on the big cherry colored couch and Bill took the chair across the room by the window.

"You come up through Santa Monica?" he asked.

"No, we came along the Coast Highway," Les said. "Why?"

"Jesus, you should have gone through Santa Monica," Bill said. "Everybody's going crazy— breaking store windows, turning cars upside down, setting fire to everything. I was down there this morning. I'm lucky I got the car back. Some jokers wanted to roll it down Wilshire Boulevard."

"What's the matter, are they crazy?" Les said. "You'd think it was the end of the world."

"For some people it is," Bill said. "What do you think M.G.M. is going to do down there, make cartoons?"

"Sure," said Les. "*Tom and Jerry in The Middle Of The Earth.*"

Bill shook his head. "Business is going out of its

mind," he said. "There's no place to set up everything down there. Everybody's flipping. Look at that paper."

Les leaned forward and took the newspaper off the coffee table. It was three days old. The main stories, of course, covered the details of the descent—the entry schedules at the various entrances: the one in Hollywood, the one in Reseda, the one in Downtown Los Angeles. In large type across eight columns, the front page headline read: *Remember! The Bomb Falls At Sunset!* Newspapers had been carrying the warning for a week. And tomorrow was the day.

The rest of the stories were about robbery, rape, arson, and murder.

"People just can't take it," Bill said. "They have to flip."

"Sometimes I feel like flipping myself," said Les.

"Why?" Bill said with a shrug. "So we live under the ground instead of over it. What the hell will change? Television will still be lousy."

"Don't tell me we aren't even leaving that above ground?"

"No, didn't you see?" Bill said. He pushed up and walked over to the coffee table. He picked up the paper Les had dropped. "Where the hell is it?" he muttered to himself, ruffling through the pages.

"There." Bill held out the paper.

TELEVISION TO GO ON
SCIENTISTS PROMISE

"Consolation?" Les said.

"Sure," Bill said, tossing down the paper. "Now we'll be able to watch the bomb smear us."

He went back to his chair.

Les shook his head. "Who's going to build television sets down there?"

"Kid, there'll be everything down—what's up, beautiful?"

Ruth stood in the archway that opened on the living room.

"Anybody want wine?" she asked. "Beer?"

Bill said beer and Les said wine, then Bill went on.

"Maybe that promise of television is a little far-fetched," he said. "But, otherwise, there'll be business as usual. Oh, maybe it'll be on a different level, but it'll be there. Christ, somebody's gonna want something for all the money they've invested in The Tunnels."

"Isn't their life enough?"

Bill went on talking about what he'd read concerning life in The Tunnels—the exchange setup, the transportation system, the plans for substitute food production and all the endless skein of details that went into the creation of a new society in a new world.

Les didn't listen. He sat looking past his friend at the purple and red sky that topped the shifting dark blue of the ocean. He heard the steady flow of Bill's words without their content; he heard the women moving in the kitchen. What *would* it be like?—he wondered. Nothing like this. No aquamarine broadloom, wall to wall, no vivid colors, no fireplace with copper screening, most of all no picture windows with the beautiful world outside for them to watch. He felt his throat tighten slowly. Tomorrow and tomorrow and tomorrow—

Ruth came in with the glasses and handed Bill his beer and Les his wine. Her eyes met those of her husband for a moment and she smiled. He wanted to pull her down suddenly and bury his face in her hair. He wanted to forget. But she returned to the kitchen and he said "What?" to Bill's question.

"I said I guess we'll go to the Reseda entrance."

"I guess it's as good as any other," Les said.

"Well, I figure the Hollywood and the downtown entrances will be jammed," Bill said. "Christ, you really threw down that wine."

Les felt the slow warmth run down into his stomach as he put down the glass.

"This thing getting you, kid?" Bill asked.

"Isn't it getting you?"

"Oh. . ." Bill shrugged. "Who knows? Maybe I just make noise to hide what it's doing to me. I guess. I feel it for Jeannie more than anything else. She's only five."

Outside they heard a car pull up in front of the house and Mary called to say that Fred and Grace were there. Bill pressed palms on his knees and pushed up.

"Don't let it get you," he said with a grin. "You're from New York. It won't be any different from the subway."

Les made a sound of disgruntled amusement.

"Forty years in the subway," he said.

"It's not that bad," Bill said, starting out of the room. "The scientists claim they'll find some way to deradiate the country and get things growing again."

"When?"

"Maybe twenty years," Bill said, and then he went out to welcome his guests.

But how do we know what they *really* look like?" Grace said. "All the pictures they print are only artist's *conceptions* of what the living quarters are like down there. They may be *holes* in the wall for all we know."

"Don't be a knocker, kid, be a booster," Bill told her.

"Uh!" Grace grunted. "I think you're oblivious to the—*terror* of this horrible descent into the ground."

They were all in the living room full of steak and salad and biscuits and pie and coffee. Les sat on the cherry colored couch, his arm around Ruth's slender waist. Grace and Fred sat on the yellow studio couch, Mary and Bill in separate chairs. Jeannie was in bed. Warmth filtered from the fireplace where a low, steady log fire burned. Fred and Bill drank beer from cans and the rest drank wine.

"Not oblivious, kid," Bill said. "Just adjusting. We have to do it. We might as well make the best of it."

"Easily said, easily said," Grace repeated. "But I for one *certainly* don't look forward to living in those tunnels. I expect to be miserable. I don't know how Fred feels, but those are *my* sentiments. I don't think it really *matters* to Fred."

"Fred is an adjuster," Bill said. "Fred is not a knocker."

Fred smiled a little and said nothing. He was a small man sitting by his wife like a patient boy with his mother in the dentist's office.

"Oh!" Grace again. "How you can be so *blasé* about it is beyond me. How can it be *anything* but bad? No theatres, no restaurants, no traveling—"

"No beauty parlors," said Bill with a short laugh.

"*Yes,* no beauty parlors," said Grace. "If you don't think *that's* important to a woman—*well.*"

"We'll have our loved ones," Mary said. "I think that's most important. And we'll all be alive."

Grace shrugged. "All right we'll be alive, we'll be together," she said. "But I'm afraid I just can't call *that* life—living in a *cellar* the rest of my life."

"Don't go," Bill said. "Show 'em how tough you are."

"*Very* funny," Grace said.

"I bet some people *will* decide not to go down there," Les said.

"If they're *crazy,*" said Grace. "Uh! What a *hideous* way to die."

"Maybe it'd be better than going underground," Bill said, "Who knows? Maybe a lot of people will spend a quiet day at home tomorrow."

"*Quiet?*" said Grace, "Don't worry, Fred and I will be down in those tunnels bright and early tomorrow."

"I'm not worried," said Bill.

They were quiet for a moment, then Bill said, "The Reseda entrance all right with everybody? We might as well decide now."

Fred made a small palms-up gesture with his hands.

"All right with me," he said. "Whatever the majority decides."

"Kid, let's face it," Bill said. "You're the most

important person we've got here. An electrician's going to be a big man down there."

Fred smiled. "That's okay," he said, "Anything you decide."

"You know," Bill said. "I wonder what the hell we mailmen are going to do down there."

"And we bank tellers," Les said.

"Oh, there'll be money down there," Bill said. "Where America goes, money goes. Now what about the car? We can only take one for six. Shall we take mine? It's the biggest."

"Why not *ours?*" Grace said.

"Doesn't matter a damn to me," Bill said. "We can't take them down with us, anyway."

Grace stared bitterly at the fire, her frail hands opening and closing in her lap.

"Oh, why don't we *stop* the bomb! Why don't we attack *first?*"

"We can't stop it now," Les said.

"I wonder if they have tunnels too," said Mary.

"Sure," Bill said, "They're probably sitting in their houses right now just like us, drinking wine and wondering what it'll be like to go underground."

"Not *them,*" Grace said, bitterly, "What do *they* care?"

Bill smiled dryly. "They care."

"There doesn't seem any point," Ruth said.

Then they all sat in silence watching their last fire of a cool California evening. Ruth rested her head on Les's shoulder as he slowly stroked her blond hair. Bill and Mary caught each other's eye and smiled a little. Fred sat and stared with gentle, melancholy eyes at the glowing logs while Grace opened up and closed her hands and looked very old.

And, outside, the stars shown down for a million times the millionth year.

Ruth and Les were sitting on their living room floor listening to records when Bill sounded his horn. For a moment they looked at each other without a word, a little frightened, the sunlight filtering between the blinds and falling like golden ladders across their legs. What can I say?—he wondered suddenly—Are there any words in the world that can make this minute easier for her?

Ruth moved against him quickly and they clung together as hard as they could. Outside the horn blew again.

"We'd better go," Les said quietly.

"All right," she said.

They stood up and Les went to the front door.

"We'll be right out!" he called.

Ruth moved into the bedroom and got their coats and the two small suitcases they were allowed to take. All their furniture, their clothes, their books, their records—they had to be left behind.

When she went back to the living room, Les was turning off the record player.

"I wish we could take more books," he said.

"They'll have libraries, honey," she said.

"I know," he said. "It just—isn't the same."

He helped her on with her coat and she helped him on with his. The apartment was very quiet and warm.

"It's so nice," she said.

He looked at her a moment as if in question, then, hurriedly, he picked up the suitcases and opened the door.

"Come on baby," he said.

At the door she turned and looked back. Abruptly she walked over to the record player and turned it on. She stood there motionlessly until the music sounded, then she went back to the door and closed it firmly behind them.

"Why did you do that?" Les asked.

She took his arm and they started down the path to the car.

"I don't know," she said, "Maybe I just want to leave our home as if it was alive."

A soft breeze blew against them as they walked and, overhead, palm trees swayed their ponderous leaves.

"It's a nice day," she said.

"Yes, it is," he said and her fingers tightened on his arm.

Bill opened the door for them.

"Hop in kids," he said. "And we'll get rolling."

Jeannie got on her knees on the front seat and talked to Les and Ruth as the car started up the street. Ruth turned and watched the apartment house disappear.

"I felt the same way about our house," Mary said.

"Don't fret, Ma," Bill said. "We'll make out down thar."

"What's *down thar?*" Jeannie asked.

"God knows," said Bill, then, "Daddy's joking baby. Down thar means down *there.*"

"Say Bill, do you think we'll be living near each other in The Tunnels?" Les asked.

"I don't know, kid," Bill said. "It goes by district. *We'll* be pretty close together I guess, but Fred and Grace won't, living way the hell over in Venice the way they do."

"I can't say I'm sorry," Mary said. "I don't relish the idea of listening to Grace complain for the next twenty years."

"Oh, Grace is all right," Bill said. "All she needs is a good swift kick where it counts once in a while."

Traffic was heavy on the main boulevards that ran east for the two city entrances. Bill drove slowly along Lincoln Boulevard toward Venice. Outside of Jeannie's chattering none of them spoke. Ruth and Les sat close to each other, hands clasped, eyes straight ahead. Today, the words kept running through his mind: *we're going underground, we're going underground today.*

At first nothing happened when Bill honked the horn. Then the front door of the little house jerked open and Grace came running wildly across the broad lawn, still wearing her dressing gown and slippers, her grey-black hair hanging down in long braids.

"Oh my God, what's happened?" Mary said as Bill pushed quickly from the car to meet Grace. He pulled open the gate in time to catch Grace as one of her slipper heels dug into the soft earth throwing her off balance.

"What's *wrong?*" he asked, bracing her with his hands.

"It's *Fred!*" she cried.

Bill's face went blank and his gaze jumped suddenly to the house standing silent and white in the sunshine. Les and Mary got out of the car quickly.

"What's wrong with—" Bill started, cutting off his words nervously.

"He won't go!" Grace cried, her face a mask of twisted fright.

They found him as Grace said he'd been all morning—fists clenched, sitting motionless in his easy chair by the window that overlooked the garden. Bill walked over to him and laid a hand on his thin shoulder.

"What's up, buddy?" he asked.

Fred looked up, a smile starting at the corners of his small mouth. "Hi," he said quietly.

"You're not going?" Bill asked.

Fred took a breath and seemed about to say something else, then he stopped. "No," he said as if he were politely refusing peas at dinner.

"Oh, my God, I *told* you, I *told* you!" Grace sobbed. "He's *insane!*"

"All right Grace, *take it easy.*" Bill snapped irritably and she pressed the soaked handkerchief to her mouth. Mary put her arm around Grace.

"Why not, pal?" Bill asked his friend.

Another smile twitched momentarily on Fred's lips. He shrugged slightly.

"Don't want to," he said.

"Oh, Fred, Fred, how can you *do* this to me?" Grace moaned, standing nervously by the front door, right hand to her throat. Bill's mouth tightened but he kept his eyes on Fred's motionless face.

"What about Grace?" he asked.

"Grace should go," Fred answered. "I want her to go, I don't want her to die."

"How can I live down there *alone?*" Grace sobbed.

Fred didn't answer, he just sat there looking straight ahead as if he felt embarrassed by all this attention, as if he was trying to gather in his mind the right thing to say.

"Look," he started, "I know this is terrible and—and it's arrogant—but I just can't go down there."

His mouth grew firm. "I won't," he said.

Bill straightened up with a weary breath.

"Well," he said helplessly.

"I—" Fred had opened up his right fist and was uncrumpling a small square of paper. "Maybe—this will say—say what I mean."

Bill took it and read it. Then he looked down at Fred and patted his shoulder once.

"Okay pal," he said and he put the paper in his coat. He looked at Grace.

"Get dressed if you're coming," he said.

"Fred!" she almost screamed his name. "Are you want to stay with him?"

"Your husband is staying," Bill told her. "Do you want to stay with him?"

"I don't want to *die!"*

Bill looked at her a moment, then turned away.

"Mary, help her dress," he said.

While they went to the car, Grace sobbing and stumbling on Mary's arm, Fred stood in the front doorway and watched his wife leave. She hadn't kissed him or embraced him, only retreated from his goodbye with a sob of angry fear. He stood there without moving a muscle and the breeze ruffled his thin hair.

When they were all in the car Bill took the paper out of his pocket.

"I'm going to read you what your husband wrote," he said flatly and he read: *"If a man dies with sun in his eyes, he dies a man. If a man goes with dirt in his nose— he only dies."*

Grace looked at Bill with bleak eyes, her hands twisting endlessly in her lap.

"Mama, why isn't Uncle Fred coming?" Jeannie asked as Bill started the car and made a sharp U turn.

"He wants to stay," was all Mary said.

The car picked up speed and headed toward Lincoln Boulevard. None of them spoke and Les thought of Fred sitting back there alone in his little house, waiting. *Alone.* The thought made his throat catch and he gritted his teeth. Was there another poem beginning in Fred's mind now, he thought, one that started—*If a man dies and there is no one there to hold his hand—*

"Oh *stop* it, stop the car!" Grace cried.

Bill pulled over to the curb.

"I don't want to go down there alone," Grace said miserably, "It's not fair to make me go alone. I—"

She stopped talking and bit her lip. "Oh—" She leaned over. "Goodbye Mary," she said and she kissed her. "Goodbye Ruth," and kissed her. Then Les and Jeannie, and she managed a brief, rueful smile at Bill.

"I hate you," she said.

"I *love* you," he answered.

They watched her go back down the block, first walking, then, as she got nearer to the house, half running with a childlike excitement. They saw Fred come to the gate and then Bill started the car and he drove away and they were alone together.

"You'd never think Fred felt that way, would you?" Les said.

"I don't know, kid," Bill said. "He always used to stay in his garden when he wasn't working. He liked to wear a pair of shorts and a tee shirt and let the sun fall on him while he trimmed the hedges or mowed the lawn or something. I can understand him feeling the way he does. If he wants to die that way, why not? He's old enough to know what he wants." He grinned. "It's Grace that surprises me."

"Don't you think it was a little unfair of him sort of—*pushing* Grace into staying with him?" Ruth asked.

"What's fair or unfair?" Bill said. "It's a man's life and a man's love. Where's the book that tells a man how to die and how to love?"

He turned the car onto Lincoln Boulevard.

They reached the entrance a little after noon and one of the hundreds in the concentrated police force directed them to the field down the road and told them to park there and walk back.

"Jesus, would you look at those cars," Bill said as he drove slowly along the road that was thick with walking people.

Cars, thousands of them. Les thought of the field he'd seen once after the second world war. It had been filled with bombers, wing to wing as far as the eye could see. This was just like it, only these were cars and the war wasn't over, it was just beginning.

"Isn't it dangerous to leave all these cars here?" Ruth asked. "Won't it make a target?"

"Kid, no matter where the bomb falls it's going to smear everything," Bill said.

"Besides," said Les, "the way the entrances are built I don't think it matters much where the bomb lands."

They all got out and stood for a moment as if they weren't sure exactly what to do. Then Bill said, "Well, let's go," and patted the hood of his car. "So long clunk—R.I.P."

"In pieces?" Les said.

There were long lines at each of the twenty desks

before the entrance. People filed slowly by and gave their names and addresses and were assigned to various bunker rows. They didn't talk much, they just held their suitcases and moved along with little steps toward the entrance to The Tunnels.

Ruth held Les's arm with clenched fingers and he felt a tautness growing around the edges of his stomach, as if the muscles there were slowly calcifying. Each short, undramatic step took them closer to the entrance, further from the sky and the sun and the stars and the moon. And suddenly Les felt very sick and very afraid. He wanted to grab Ruth's hand and drive back to their apartment and stay there till it ended. Fred was right— he couldn't help feeling it. Fred was right to know that a man couldn't leave the only home he'd ever had and burrow into the earth like a mole and still be himself. Something would happen down there, something would change. The artificial air, the even banks of bulbed sunshine, the electric moon and the fluorescent stars invented at the behest of some psychological study that foretold aberration if they were taken away completely. Did they suppose these things would be enough? Could they possibly believe that a man might crawl beneath the ground in one great living grave for twenty years and keep his soul?

He felt his body tighten involuntarily and he wanted to scream out at all the stupidity in the world that made men scourge themselves before their own whips to their own destruction in one endless chain of blind sadisms. His breath caught and he glanced at Ruth and saw that she was looking at him.

"Are you all right?"

He drew in a shaking breath. "Yes," he said, "All right."

He tried to numb his mind but without success. He kept looking at all the people around him, wondering if they felt as he did this fierce anger at what was happening, at what, basically, they had allowed to happen. Did they think too of the night before, of the stars and the crisp air and the sounds of earth? He shook his head. It was torture to think about them.

He looked over at Bill as the five of them shuffled slowly down the long concrete ramp to the elevators. Bill was holding Jeannie's hand in his, looking down at her without any expression on his face. Then Les saw him turn and nudge Mary with the suitcase he held in his other hand. Mary looked at him and Bill winked.

"Where are we going, papa?" Jeannie asked, and her voice echoed shrilly off the white tile walls.

Bill's throat moved. "I told you," he replied. "We're going to live under the ground a while."

"How long?" Jeannie asked.

"Don't talk anymore baby," Bill said. "I don't know."

There was no sound in the elevator. There were a hundred people in it and it was as still as a tomb as it went down. And down. And down.

Deadline

THERE ARE AT least two nights a year a doctor doesn't plan on and those are Christmas Eve and New Year's Eve. On Christmas Eve it was Bobby Dascouli's arm burns. I was salving and swathing them about the time I would have been nestled in an easy chair with Ruth eyeing the technicolor doings of the Christmas tree.

So it came as small surprise that ten minutes after we got to my sister Mary's house for the New Year's Eve party my answering service phoned and told me there was an emergency call downtown.

Ruth smiled at me sadly and shook her head. She kissed me on the cheek. "Poor Bill," she said.

"Poor Bill indeed," I said, putting down my first drink of the evening, two-thirds full. I patted her much evident stomach.

"Don't have that baby till I get back," I told her.

"I'll do my bestest," she said.

I gave hurried goodbyes to everyone and left; turning up the collar of my overcoat and crunching over the snow-packed walk to the Ford; milking the choke and finally getting the engine started. Driving downtown with that look of dour reflection I've seen on many a GP's face at many a time.

It was after eleven when my tire chains rattled onto the dark desertion of East Main Street. I drove three blocks north to the address and parked in front of what

52

had been a refined apartment dwelling when my father was in practice. Now it was a boardinghouse, ancient, smelling of decay.

In the vestibule I lined the beam of my pencil flashlight over the mail boxes but couldn't find the name. I rang the landlady's bell and stepped over to the hall door. When the buzzer sounded I pushed it open.

At the end of the hall a door opened and a heavy woman emerged. She wore a black sweater over her wrinkled green dress, striped anklets over her heavy stockings, saddle shoes over the anklets. She had no makeup on; the only color in her face was a chapped redness in her cheeks. Wisps of steel-gray hair hung across her temples. She picked at them as she trundled down the dim hallway toward me.

"You the doctor?" she asked.

I said I was.

"I'm the one called ya," she said. "There's an old guy up the fourth floor says he's dyin'."

"What room?" I asked.

"I'll show ya."

I followed her wheezing ascent up the stairs. We stopped in front of room 47 and she rapped on the thin paneling of the door, then pushed it open.

"In here," she said.

As I entered I saw him lying on an iron bed. His body had the flaccidity of a discarded doll. At his sides, frail hands lay motionless, topographed with knots of vein, islanded with liver spots. His skin was the brown of old page edges, his face a wasted mask. On the caseless pillow, his head lay still, its white hair straggling across the stripes like threading drifts of snow. There was a pallid stubble on his cheeks. His pale blue eyes were fixed on the ceiling.

As I slipped off my hat and coat I saw that there was no suffering evident. His expression was one of peaceful acceptance. I sat down on the bed and took his wrist. His eyes shifted and he looked at me.

"Hello," I said smiling.

"Hello." I was surprised by the cognizance in his voice.

The beat of his blood was what I expected however—a bare trickle of life, a pulsing almost lost beneath the fingers. I put down his hand and laid my palm across his forehead. There was no fever. But then he wasn't sick. He was only running down.

I patted the old man's shoulder and stood, gesturing toward the opposite side of the room. The landlady clumped there with me.

"How long has he been in bed?" I asked.

"Just since this afternoon," she said. "He come down to my room and said he was gonna die tonight."

I stared at her. I'd never come in contact with such a thing. I'd read about it; everyone has. An old man or woman announces that, at a certain time, they'll die and, when the time comes, they do. Who knows what it is; will or prescience or both. All one knows is that it is a strangely awesome thing.

"Has he any relatives?" I asked.

"None I know of," she said.

I nodded.

"Don't understand it," she said.

"What?"

"When he first moved in about a month ago he was all right. Even this afternoon he didn't look sick."

"You never know," I said.

"No. You don't." There was a haunted and uneasy flickering back deep in her eyes.

"Well, there's nothing I can do for him," I said. "He's not in pain. It's just a matter of time."

The landlady nodded.

"How old is he?" I asked.

"He never said."

"I see." I walked back to the bed.

"I heard you," the old man told me.

"Oh?"

"You want to know how old I am."

"How old are you?"

He started to answer, then began coughing dryly. I saw a glass of water on the bedside table and, sitting, I propped the old man while he drank a little. Then I put him down again.

"I'm one year old," he said.

It didn't register. I stared down at his calm face. Then, smiling nervously, I put the glass down on the table.

"You don't believe that," he said.

"Well—" I shrugged.

"It's true enough," he said.

I nodded and smiled again.

"I was born on December 31st, 1958," he said, "At midnight."

He closed his eyes. "What's the use?" he said, "I've told a hundred people and none of them understood."

"Tell me about it," I said.

After a few moments, he drew in breath, slowly.

"A week after I was born," he said, "I was walking and talking. I was eating by myself. My mother and father couldn't believe their eyes. They took me to a doctor. I don't know what he thought but he didn't do anything. What could he do? I wasn't sick. He sent me home with my mother and father. Precocious growth, he said.

"In another week we were back again. I remember my mother's and father's faces when we drove there. They were afraid of me.

"The doctor didn't know what to do. He called in specialists and they didn't know what to do. I was a normal four-year-old boy. They kept me under observation. They wrote papers about me. I didn't see my father and mother any more."

The old man stopped a moment, then went on in the same mechanical way.

"In another week I was six," he said. "In another week, eight. Nobody understood. They tried everything but there was no answer. And I was ten and twelve. I was fourteen and I ran away because I was sick of being stared at."

He looked at the ceiling for almost a minute.

"You want to hear more?" he asked then.

"Yes," I said, automatically. I was amazed at how easily he spoke.

"In the beginning I tried to fight it," he said. "I went to doctors and screamed at them. I told them to find out what was wrong with me. But there wasn't anything wrong with me. I was just getting two years older every week.

"Then I got the idea."

I started a little, twitching out of the reverie of staring at him. "Idea?" I asked.

"This is how the story got started," the old man said.

"What story?"

"About the old year and the new year," he said. "The old year is an old man with a beard and a scythe. You know. And the new year is a little baby."

The old man stopped. Down in the street I heard a tire-screeching car turn a corner and speed past the building.

"I think there have been men like me all through time," the old man said. "Men who live for just a year. I don't know how it happens or why; but, once in a while, it does. That's how the story got started. After a while, people forgot how it started. They think it's a fable now. They think it's symbolic; but it isn't."

The old man turned his worn face toward the wall.

"And I'm 1959," he said, quietly. "That's who I am."

The landlady and I stood in silence looking down at him. Finally, I glanced at her. Abruptly, as if caught in guilt, she turned and hurried across the floor. The door thumped shut behind her.

I looked back at the old man. Suddenly, my breath

seemed to stop. I leaned over and picked up his hand. There was no pulse. Shivering, I put down his hand and straightened up. I stood looking down at him. Then, from where I don't know, a chill laced up my back. Without thought, I extended my left hand and the sleeve of my coat slid back across my watch.

To the second.

I drove back to Mary's house unable to get the old man's story out of my mind—or the weary acceptance in his eyes. I kept telling myself it was only a coincidence, but I couldn't quite convince myself.

Mary let me in. The living room was empty.

"Don't tell me the party's broken up already?" I said.

Mary smiled. "Not broken up," she said, "Just continued at the hospital."

I stared at her, my mind swept blank. Mary took my arm.

"And you'll never guess," she said, "what time Ruth had the sweetest little boy."

The Man Who
Made the World

DOCTOR JANISHEFSKY SAT in his office. *Leaning back in a great leather chair, hands folded. He had a reflective air and a well-trimmed goatee. He hummed a few bars of*—"It Ain't Whatcha Do, It's The Way Thatcha Do, It's The Way Thatcha Do It." *He broke off and looked up with a kindly smile as the nurse entered. Her name was Mudde.*

NURSE MUDDE: Doctor, there is a man in the waiting room who says he made the world.

DOCTOR J: Oh?

NURSE MUDDE: Shall I let him in?

DOCTOR J: By all means, Nurse Mudde. Show the man in. *Nurse Mudde left. A small man entered. He was five foot five wearing a suit made for a man six foot five. His hands were near-hidden by the sleeve ends, his trouser leg bottoms creased sharply at the shoe tops, assuming the function of unattached spats. The shoes were virtually invisible. As was the gentleman's mouth lurking behind a mustache of mouselike proportions.*

DOCTOR J: Won't you have a seat Mr.—

SMITH: Smith. (*He sits*)

DOCTOR J: Now.

(*They regard each other*)

DOCTOR J: My nurse tells me you made the world.

SMITH Yes. (*In a confessional tone*) I did.

DOCTOR J: (*Settling back in his chair*) All of it?

SMITH: Yes.

DOCTOR J: And everything in it?

SMITH: Take a little, give a little.

DOCTOR J: You're sure of this?

SMITH: (*With an expression that clearly says—I am telling the truth the whole truth and nothing but the truth so help me.*) Quite sure.

DOCTOR J: (*Nods once*) When did you do this thing?

SMITH: Five years ago.

DOCTOR J: How old are you?

SMITH: Forty-seven.

DOCTOR J: Where were you the other forty-two years?

SMITH: I wasn't.

DOCTOR J: You mean you started out—

SMITH: Forty-two years old. That's correct.

DOCTOR J: But the world is millions of years old.

SMITH: (*Shaking his head*) No. It isn't.

DOCTOR J: It's five years old.

SMITH: That's correct.

DOCTOR J: What about fossils? What about the age of rocks? Uranium into lead. What about diamonds?

SMITH: (*Not to be bothered*) Illusions.

DOCTOR J: You made them up.

SMITH: That's—

DOCTOR J: (*Breaking in*) Why?

SMITH: To see if I could.

DOCTOR J: I don't—

SMITH: Anyone can make a world. It takes ingenuity to make one and then make the people on it think it's existed for millions of years.

DOCTOR J: How long did all this take you?

SMITH: Three and a half months. World time.

DOCTOR J: What do you mean by that?

SMITH: Before I made the world I lived beyond time.

DOCTOR J: Where's that?

SMITH: No where.

DOCTOR J: In the cosmos?

SMITH: That's correct.

DOCTOR J: You didn't like it there?

SMITH: No. It was boring.

DOCTOR J: And that's why—

SMITH: I made the world.

DOCTOR J: Yes. But—how did you make it?

SMITH: I had books.

DOCTOR J: Books?

SMITH: Instruction books.

DOCTOR J: Where did you get them?

SMITH: I made them up.

DOCTOR J: You mean you wrote them?

SMITH: I—made them up.

DOCTOR J: How?

SMITH: (*Mustache bristling truculently*) I made them up.

DOCTOR J: (*Lips pursed*) So there you were out in the cosmos with a handful of books.

SMITH: That's correct.

DOCTOR J: What if you had dropped them?

SMITH: (*Chooses not to answer this patent absurdity*)

DOCTOR J: Mister Smith.

SMITH: Yes?

DOCTOR J: Who made you?

SMITH: (*Shakes his head*) I don't know.

DOCTOR J: Were you always like this? (*He points at Mr. Smith's lowly frame.*)

SMITH: I don't think so. I think that I was punished.

DOCTOR J: For what?

SMITH: For making the world so complicated.

DOCTOR J: I should think so.

SMITH: It's not my fault. I just made it, I didn't say it would work right.

DOCTOR J: You just started your machine and then walked away.

SMITH: That's—

DOCTOR J: Then what are you doing here?

SMITH: I told you. I think I've been punished.

DOCTOR J: Oh yes. For making it too complicated. I forgot.

SMITH: That's correct.

DOCTOR J: Who punished you?

SMITH: I don't remember.

DOCTOR J: That's convenient.

SMITH: (*Looks morose*)

DOCTOR J: Might it be God?

SMITH: (*Shrugs*) It might.

DOCTOR J: He might have a few fingers in the rest of the universe.

SMITH: He might. But I made the world.

DOCTOR J: Enough, Mr. Smith, you did not make the world.

SMITH: (*Insulted*) Yes, I did too.

DOCTOR J: And you created me?

SMITH: (*Concedingly*) Indirectly.

DOCTOR J: Then uncreate me?

SMITH: I can't.

DOCTOR J: Why?

SMITH: I just started things. I don't control them now.

DOCTOR J: (*Sighs*) Then what are you worried about, Mr. Smith?

SMITH: I have a premonition.

DOCTOR J: What about?

SMITH: I'm going to die.

DOCTOR J: So—?

SMITH: Someone has to take over. Or else—

DOCTOR J: Or else—?

SMITH: The whole world will go.

DOCTOR J: Go where?

SMITH: No where. Just disappear.

DOCTOR J: How can it disappear if it works independently of you?

SMITH: It will be taken away to punish me.

DOCTOR J: You?

SMITH: Yes.

DOCTOR J: You mean if you die, the entire world will disappear?

SMITH: That's correct.

DOCTOR J: If I shot you, the instant you died I would disappear?

SMITH: That's—

DOCTOR J: I have advice.

SMITH: Yes? You will help?

DOCTOR J: Go to see a reputable psychiatrist.

SMITH: (*Standing*) I should have known. I have no more to say.

DOCTOR J: (*Shrugs*) As you will.

SMITH: I'll go but you'll be sorry about this.

DOCTOR J: I dare say you are already sorry, Mr. Smith.

SMITH: Goodbye. (*Mr. Smith exits. Doctor Janishefsky calls for his nurse over the interphone. Nurse Mudde enters.*)

NURSE M: Yes, doctor?

DOCTOR J: Nurse Mudde, stand by the window and tell me what you see.

NURSE M: What I—?

DOCTOR J: What you see. I want you to tell me what Mr. Smith does after he comes out of the building.

NURSE M: (*Shrugs*) Yes, doctor. (*She goes to the window*)

DOCTOR J: Has he come out yet?

NURSE M: No.

DOCTOR J: Keep watching.

NURSE M: There he is. He's stepping off the curb. He's walking across the street.

DOCTOR J: Yes.

NURSE M: He's stopping now in the middle of the street. He's turning. He's looking up at this window. There's a look of—of—*realization* on his face. He's coming back. (*She screams*) He's been hit by a car. He's lying on the street.

DOCTOR J: What is it, Nurse Mudde?

NURSE M: (*Reeling*) Everything is—is *fading!* Doctor Janishefsky, it's fading! (*Another scream*)

DOCTOR J: Don't be absurd, Nurse Mudde. Look at

me. Can you honestly say that—(*He stops talking. She cannot honestly say anything. She is not there. Doctor Janishefsky, who is not really Doctor Janishefsky, floats alone in the cosmos in his chair, which is not really a chair. He looks at the chair beside him.*) I hope you've learned your lesson. I'm going to put your toy back but don't you dare go near it. So you're bored are you? Scalliwag! You just behave yourself or I'll take away your books too! (*He snorts.*) So you made them up, did you? (He looks around) How about picking them up, jackanapes!

SMITH: (*Who is not really Smith*) Yes, father.

Graveyard Shift

DEAR PA:

I am sending you this note under Rex's collar because I got to stay here. I hope the note gets to you all right.

I couldn't deliver the tax letter you sent me with because the Widow Blackwell is killed. She is upstairs. I put her on her bed. She looks awful. I wish you would get the sheriff and the coronir Wilks.

Little Jim Blackwell, I don't know where he is right now. He is so scared he goes running around the house and hiding from me. He must have got awful scared by whoever killed his ma. He don't say a word. He just runs around like a scared rat. I see his eyes sometimes in the dark and then they are gone. They got no electric power here you know.

I came out toward sundown bringing that note. I rung the bell but there wasn't no answer so I pushed open the front door and looked in.

All the shades was down. And I heard someone running light in the front room and then feet running upstairs. I called around for the Widow but she didn't answer me.

I started upstairs and saw Jim looking down through the bannister posts. When he saw me looking at him, he run down the hall and I ain't seen him since.

I looked around the upstairs rooms. Finally, I went in the Widow Blackwell's room and there she was dead on the floor in a puddle of blood. Her throat was cut and her eyes was wide open and looking up at me. It was an awful sight.

I shut her eyes and searched around some and I found the razor. The Widow has all her clothes on so I figure it were only robbery that the killer meant.

Well, Pa, please come out quick with the sheriff and the coronir Wilks. I will stay here and watch to see that Jim don't go running out of the house and maybe get lost in the woods. But come as fast as you can because I don't like sitting here with her up there like that and Jim sneaking around in the dark house.

LUKE

DEAR GEORGE:

We just got back from your sister's house. We haven't told the papers yet so I'll have to be the one to let you know.

I sent Luke out there with a property tax note and he found your sister murdered. I don't like to be the one to tell you but somebody has to. The sheriff and his boys are scouring the countryside for the killer. They figure it was a tramp or something. She wasn't raped though and, far as we can tell, nothing was stolen.

What I mean more to tell you about is little Jim.

That boy is fixing to die soon from starvation and just plain scaredness. He won't eat nothing. Sometimes, he gulps down a piece of bread or a piece of candy but as soon as he starts to chewing his face gets all twisted and he gets violent sick and throws up. I don't understand it at all.

Luke found your sister in her room with her throat cut ear to ear. Coronor Wilks says it was a strong, steady hand that done it because the cut is deep and sure. I am terrible sorry to be the one to tell you all this but I think it is better you know. The funeral will be in a week.

Luke and I had a long time rounding up the boy. He was like lightning. He ran around in the dark and squealed like a rat. He showed his teeth at us when we'd corner him with a lantern. His skin is all white and the way he rolls his eyes back and foams at his mouth is something awful to see.

We finally caught him. He bit us and squirmed around like a eel. Then he got all stiff and it was like carrying a two-by-four, Luke said.

We took him into the kitchen and tried to give him something to eat. He wouldn't take a bite. He gulped down some milk like he felt guilty about it. Then, in a second, his face twists and he draws back his lips and the milk comes out.

He kept trying to run away from us. Never a single word out of him. He just squeaks and mutters like a monkey talking to itself.

We finally carried him upstairs to put him to bed. He froze soon as we touched him and I thought his eyes would fall out he opened them so wide. His jaw fell slack and he stared at us like we was boogie men or trying to slice open his throat like his ma's.

He wouldn't go into his room. He screamed and twisted in our hands like a fish. He braced his feet against the wall and tugged and pulled and scratched. We had to slap his face and then his eyes got big and he got like a board again and we carried him in his room.

When I took off his clothes, I got a shock like I haven't had in years, George. That boy is all scars and bruises on his back and chest like someone has strung him up and tortured him with pliers or hot iron or God knows what all. I got a downright chill seeing that. I know they said the widow wasn't the same in her head after her husband died, but I can't believe she done this. It is the work of a crazy person.

Jim was sleepy but he wouldn't shut his eyes. He kept looking around the ceiling and the window and his lips kept moving like he was trying to talk. He was moaning kind of low and shaky when Luke and I went out in the hall.

No sooner did we leave him than he's screaming at the top of his voice and thrashing in his bed like someone was strangling him. We rushed in and I held the lantern high but we couldn't see anything. I thought the boy was sick with fear and seeing things.

Then, as if it was meant to happen, the lantern ran out of oil and all of a sudden we saw white faces staring at us from the walls and ceiling and the window.

It was a shaky minute there, George, with the kid screaming out his lungs and twisting on his bed but never getting up. And Luke trying to find the door and me feeling for a match but trying to look at those horrible faces at the same time.

Finally I found a match and I got it lit and we couldn't see the faces any more, just part of one on the window.

I sent Luke down to the car for some oil and when he come back we lit the lantern again and looked at the window and saw that the face was painted on it so's to light up in the dark. Same thing for the faces on the walls and the ceiling. It was enough to scare a man out of half his wits to think of anybody doing that inside a little boy's room.

We took him to another room and put him down to bed. When we left him he was squirming in his sleep and muttering words we couldn't understand. I left Luke in the hall outside the room to watch. I went and looked around the house some more.

In the Widow's room I found a whole shelf of psychology books. They was all marked in different places. I looked in one place and it told about a thing how they can make rats go crazy by making them think there is food in a place when there isn't. And another one about how they can make a dog lose its appetite and starve to death by hitting big pieces of pipe together at the same time when the dog is trying to eat.

I guess you know what I think. But it is so terrible I

can hardly believe it. I mean that Jim might have got so
crazy that he cut her. He is so small I don't see how he
could.

You are her only living kin, George, and I think you
should do something about the boy. We don't want to
put him in a orphan home. He is in no shape for it. That
is why I am telling you all about him so you can judge.

There was another thing. I played a record on a
phonograph in the boy's room. It sounded like wild
animals all making terrible noises and even louder than
them was a terrible high laughing.

That is about all, George. We will let you know if the
sheriff finds the one who killed your sister because no
one really believes that Jim could have done it. I wish
you would take the boy and try to fix him up.

Until I hear,

                                        SAM DAVIS

DEAR SAM:

I got your letter and am more upset than I can say.

I knew for a long time that my sister was mentally
unbalanced after her husband's death, but I had no
idea in the world she was so far gone.

You see, when she was a girl she fell in love with Phil.
There was never anyone else in her life. The sun rose
and descended on her love for him. She was so jealous
that, once, because he had taken another girl to a party,
she crashed her hands through a window and nearly
bled to death.

Finally, Phil married her. There was never a happier
couple, it seemed. She did anything and everything for
him. He was her whole life.

When Jim was born I went to see her at the hospital.
She told me she wished it had been born dead because
she knew that the boy meant so much to Phil and she
hated to have Phil want anything but her.

She never was good to Jim. She always resented him.
And, that day, three years ago, when Phil drowned
saving Jim's life, she went out of her mind. I was with

her when she heard about it. She ran into the kitchen and got a carving knife and took it running through the streets, trying to find Jim so she could kill him. She finally fainted in the road and we took her home.

She wouldn't even look at Jim for a month. Then she packed up and took him to that house in the woods. Since then I never saw her.

You saw yourself, the boy is terrified of everyone and everything. Except one person. My sister planned that. Step by step she planned it—God help me for never realizing it before. In a whole, monstrous world of horrors she built around that boy she left him trust and need for only one person—*her*. She was Jim's only shield against those horrors. She knew that, when she died, Jim would go completely mad because there wouldn't be anyone in the world he could turn to for comfort.

I think you see now why I say there isn't any murderer.

Just bury her quick and send the boy to me. I'm not coming to the funeral.

GEORGE BARNES

The Likeness of Julie

October.

EDDY FOSTER HAD never noticed the girl in his English class until that day.

It wasn't because she sat behind him. Any number of times he'd glanced around while Professor Euston was writing on the blackboard or reading to them from *College Literature*. Any number of times, he'd seen her as he left or entered the classroom. Occassionally, he'd passed her in the hallways or on the campus. Once, she'd even touched him on the shoulder during class and handed him a pencil which had fallen from his pocket.

Still, he'd never noticed her the way he noticed other girls. First of all, she had no figure—or if she did she kept it hidden under loose-fitting clothes. Second, she wasn't pretty and she looked too young. Third, her voice was faint and high-pitched.

Which made it curious that he should notice her that day. All through class, he'd been thinking about the redhead in the first row. In the theatre of his mind he'd staged her—and himself—through an endless carnal play. He was just raising the curtain on another act when he heard the voice behind him.

"Professor?" it asked.

"Yes, Miss Eldridge."

Eddy glanced across his shoulder as Miss Eldridge asked a question about *Beowulf*. He saw the plainness of her little girl's face, heard her faltering voice, noticed the loose yellow sweater she was wearing. And, as he watched, the thought came suddenly to him.

Take her.

Eddy turned back quickly, his heartbeat jolting as if he'd spoken the words aloud. He repressed a grin. What a screwy idea that was. Take *her?* With no figure? With that kid's face of hers?

That was when he realized it was her face which had given him the idea. The very childishness of it seemed to needle him perversely.

There was a noise behind him. Eddy glanced back. The girl had dropped her pen and was bending down to get it. Eddy felt a crawling tingle in his flesh as he saw the strain of her bust against the tautening sweater. Maybe she had a figure after all. That was more exciting yet. A child afraid to show her ripening body. The notion struck dark fire in Eddy's mind.

Eldridge, Julie, read the year book. *St. Louis, Arts & Sciences.*

As he'd expected, she belonged to no sorority or organizations. He looked at her photograph and she seemed to spring alive in his imagination—shy, withdrawn, existing in a shell of warped repressions.

He had to have her.

Why? He asked himself the question endlessly but no logical answer ever came. Still, visions of her were never long out of his mind—the two of them locked in a cabin at the *Hiway Motel,* the wall heater crowding their lungs with oven air while they rioted in each other's flesh; he and this degraded innocent.

The bell had rung and, as the students left the classroom, Julie dropped her books.

"Here, let me pick them up," said Eddy.

"Oh." She stood motionless while he collected them. From the corners of his eyes, he saw the ivory smoothness of her legs. He shuddered and stood with the books.

"Here," he said.

"Thank you." Her eyes lowered and the faintest of color touched her cheeks. She wasn't so bad-looking, Eddy thought. And she did have a figure. Not much of one but a figure.

"What is it we're supposed to read for tomorrow?" he heard himself asking.

"The—'Wife of Bath's Tale,' isn't it?" she asked.

"Oh, is that it?" Ask her for a date, he thought.

"Yes. I think so."

He nodded. Ask her now, he thought.

"Well," said Julie. She began to turn away.

Eddy smiled remotely at her and felt his stomach muscles trembling.

"Be seeing you," he said.

He stood in the darkness staring at her window. Inside the room, the light went on as Julie came back from the bathroom. She wore a terrycloth robe and was carrying a towel, a washcloth, and a plastic soap box. Eddy watched her put the washcloth and soap box on her bureau and sit down on the bed. He stood there rigidly, watching her with eyes that did not blink. What was he doing here? he thought. If anybody caught him, he'd be arrested. He had to leave.

Julie stood. She undid the sash at her waist and the bathrobe slipped to the floor. Eddy froze. He parted his lips, sucking at the damp air. She had the body of a woman—full-hipped with breasts that both jutted and hung. And with that pretty child's face—

Eddy felt hot breath forcing out between his lips. He muttered, *"Julie, Julie, Julie—"*

Julie turned away to dress.

The idea was insane. He knew it but he couldn't get away from it. No matter how he tried to think of something else, it kept returning.

He'd invite her to a drive-in movie, drug her coke there, take her to the *Hiway Motel*. To guarantee his safety afterward, he'd take photographs of her and threaten to send them to her parents if she said anything.

The idea was insane. He knew it but he couldn't fight it. He had to do it now—now when she was still a stranger to him; an unknown female with a child's face and a woman's body. That was what he wanted; not an individual.

No! It was insane! He cut his English class twice in succession. He drove home for the weekend. He saw a lot of movies. He read magazines and took long walks. He could beat this thing.

"Miss Eldridge?"

Julie stopped. As she turned to face him, the sun made ripples on her hair. She looked very pretty, Eddy thought.

"Can I walk with you?" he asked.

"All right," she said.

They walked along the campus path.

"I was wondering," said Eddy, "if you'd like to go to the drive-in movie Friday night." He was startled at the calmness of his voice.

"Oh," said Julie. She glanced at him shyly. "What's playing?" she asked.

He told her.

"That sounds very nice," she said.

Eddy swallowed. "Good," he answered. "What time shall I pick you up?"

He wondered, later, if it made her curious that he didn't ask her where she lived.

There was a light burning on the porch of the house she roomed in. Eddy pushed the bell and waited, watching two moths flutter around the light. After several moments, Julie opened the door. She looked almost beautiful, he thought. He'd never seen her dressed so well.

"Hello," she said.

"Hi," he answered, "Ready to go?"

"I'll get my coat." She went down the hall and into her room. In there, she'd stood naked that night, her body glowing in the light. Eddy pressed his teeth together. He'd be all right. She'd never tell anyone when she saw the photographs he was going to take.

Julie came back down the hallway and they went out to the car. Eddy opened the door for her.

"Thank you," she murmured. As she sat down, Eddy caught a glimpse of stockinged knees before she pulled her skirt down. He slammed the door and walked around the car. His throat felt parched.

Ten minutes later, he nosed the car onto an empty ramp in the last row of the drive-in theatre and cut the engine. He reached outside and lifted the speaker off its pole and hooked it over the window. There was a cartoon playing.

"You want some popcorn and coke?" he asked, feeling a sudden bolt of dread that she might say no.

"Yes. Thank you," Julie said.

"I'll be right back." Eddie pushed out of the car and started for the snack bar. His legs were shaking.

He waited in the milling crowd of students, seeing only his thoughts. Again and again, he shut the cabin door and locked it, pulled the shades down, turned on all the lights, switched on the wall heater. Again and again, he walked over to where Julie lay stupefied and helpless on the bed.

"Yours?" said the attendant.

Eddy started. "Uh—two popcorns and a large and small coke." he said.

He felt himself begin to shiver convulsively. He couldn't do it. He might go to jail the rest of his life. He paid the man mechanically and moved off with the cardboard tray. The photographs, you idiot, he thought. They're your protection. He felt angry desire shudder through his body. Nothing was going to stop him. On the way back to the car, he emptied the contents of the packet into the small coke.

Julie was sitting quietly when he opened the door and slid back in. The feature had begun.

"Here's your coke," he said. He handed her the small cup with her box of popcorn.

"Thank you," said Julie.

Eddy sat watching the picture. He felt his heart thud slowly like a beaten drum. He felt bugs of perspiration running down his back and sides. The popcorn was dry and tasteless. He kept drinking coke to wet his throat. Soon now, he thought. He presses his lips together and stared at the screen. He heard Julie eating popcorn, he heard her drinking coke.

The thoughts were coming faster now: the door locked, the shades drawn, the room a bright-lit oven as they twisted on the bed together. Now they were doing things that Eddy almost never thought of—wild, demented things. It was her face, he thought; that damned angel's face of hers. It made the mind seek out every black avenue it could find.

Eddy glanced over at Julie. He felt his hands retract so suddenly that he spilled coke on his trousers. Her empty cup had fallen to the floor, the box of popcorn turned over on her lap. Her head was lying on the seat back and, for one hideous moment, Eddie thought she was dead.

Then she inhaled raspingly and turned her head toward him. He saw her tongue move, dark and sluggish, on her lips.

Suddenly, he was deadly calm again. He picked the speaker off the window and hung it up outside. He threw out the cups and boxes. He started the engine and backed out into the aisle. He turned on his parking lights and drove out of the theatre.

Hiway Motel. The sign blinked off and on a quarter of a mile away. For a second, Eddy thought he read *No Vacancy* and he made a frightened sound. Then he saw that he was wrong. he was still trembling as he circled the car around the drive and parked to one side of the office.

Bracing himself, he went inside and rang the bell. He was very calm and the man didn't say a word to him. He had Eddy fill out the registration card and gave him the key.

Eddy pulled his car in to the breezeway beside the cabin. He put his camera in the room, then went out and looked around. There was no one in sight. He ran to the car and opened the door. He carried Julie to the cabin door, his shoes crunching quickly on the gravel. He carried her into the dark room and dropped her on the bed.

Then it was his dream coming true. The door was locked. He moved around the room on quivering legs, pulling down the shades. He turned on the wall heater. He found the light switch by the door and pushed it up. He turned on all the lamps and pulled their shades off. He dropped one of them and it rolled across the rug. He left it there. He went over to where Julie lay.

In falling to the bed, her skirt had pulled-up to her thighs. He could see the tops of her stockings and the garter buttons fastened to them. Swallowing Eddie sat down and drew her up into a sitting position. He took her sweater off. Shakily, he reached around her and unhooked her bra; her breasts slipped free. Quickly, he unzipped her skirt and pulled it down.

In seconds, she was naked. Eddy propped her against the pillows, posing her, *Dear God, the body on her.* Eddy closed her eyes and shuddered. *No,* he thought, this is the important part. First get the photographs and you'll be safe. She can't do anything to you then; she'll be too scared. He stood up, tensely, and got his camera. He set the dials. He got her centered on the viewer. Then he spoke.

"Open your eyes," he said.
Julie did.

He was at her house before six the next morning,
moving up the alley cautiously and into the yard
outside her window. He hadn't slept all night. His eyes
felt dry and hot.

Julie was on her bed exactly as he'd placed her. He
looked at her a moment, his heartbeat slow and heavy.
Then he raked a nail across the screen. "Julie," he said.

She murmured indistinctly and turned onto her side.
She faced him now.

"Julie."

Her eyes fluttered open. She stared at him dazedly.
"Who's that?" she asked.

"Eddy. Let me in."

"Eddy?"

Suddenly, she caught her breath and shrank back
and he knew that she remembered.

"Let me in or you're in trouble," he muttered. He
could feel his legs begin to shake.

Julie lay motionless a few seconds, eyes fixed on his.
Then she pushed to her feet and weaved unsteadily
toward the door. Eddy turned for the alley. He strode
down it nervously and stared up the porch steps as she
came outside.

"What do you want?" she whispered. She looked
exciting, half asleep, her clothes and hair all mussed.

"Inside," he said.

Julie stiffened. "No."

"All right, come on," he said, taking her hand
roughly. "We'll talk in my car."

She walked with him to the car and, as he slid in
beside her, he saw that she was shivering.

"I'll turn on the heater," he said. It sounded stupidly
inane. He was here to threaten her, not comfort.
Angrily, he started the engine and drove away from the
curb.

"Where are we going?" Julie asked.

He didn't know at first. Then, suddenly, he thought of the place outside of town where dating students always parked. It would be deserted at this hour. Eddy felt a swollen tingling in his body and he pressed down on the accelerator. Sixteen minutes later, the car was standing in the silent woods. A pale mist hung across the ground and seemed to lap at the doors.

Julie wasn't shivering now; the inside of the car was hot.

'What is it?' she asked, faintly.

Impulsively, Eddy reached into his coat pocket and pulled out the photographs. He threw them on her lap.

Julie didn't make a sound. She just stared down at the photographs with frozen eyes, her fingers twitching as she held them.

"Just in case you're thinking of calling the police," Eddy faltered. He clenched his teeth. *Tell her!* he thought savagely. In a dull, harsh voice, he told her everything he'd done the night before. Julie's face grew pale and rigid as she listened. Her hands pressed tautly at each other. Outside, the mist appeared to rise around the windows like a chalky fluid. It surrounded them.

"You want money?" Julie whispered.

"Take off your clothes," he said. It wasn't his voice, it occurred to him. The sound of it was too malignant, too inhuman.

Then Julie whimpered and Eddy felt a surge of blinding fury boil upward in him. He jerked his hand back, saw it flail out in a blur of movement, heard the sound of it striking her on the mouth, felt the sting across his knuckles.

"Take them off!" His voice was deafening in the stifling closeness of the car. Eddy blinked and gasped for breath. He stared dizzily at Julie as, sobbing, she began to take her clothes off. There was a thread of blood trickling from a corner of her mouth. *No, don't,* he heard a voice beg in his mind. *Don't do this.* It faded

quickly as he reached for her with alien hands.

When he got home at ten that morning there was blood and skin under his nails. The sight of it made him violently ill. He lay trembling on his bed, lips quivering, eyes staring at the ceiling. I'm through, he thought. He had the photographs. He didn't have to see her anymore. Already, his brain felt like rotting sponge, so bloated with corruption that the pressure of his skull caused endless overflow into his thoughts. Trying to sleep, he thought, instead, about the bruises on her lovely body, the ragged scratches, and the bite marks. He heard her screaming in his mind.

He would not see her anymore.

December.

Julie opened her eyes and saw tiny fallen shadows on the wall. She turned her head and looked out through the window. It was beginning to snow. The whiteness of it reminded her of the morning Eddy had first shown her the photographs.

The photographs. That was what had woken her. She closed her eyes and concentrated. They were burning. She could see the prints and negatives scattered on the bottom of a large enamel pan—the kind used for developing film. Bright flames crackled on them and the enamel was smudging.

Julie held her breath. She pushed her mental gaze further—to scan the room that was lit by the flaming enamel pan—until it came to rest upon the broken thing that dangled and swayed, suspended from the closet hook.

She sighed. It hadn't lasted very long. That was the trouble with a mind like Eddy's. The very weakness which made it vulnerable to her soon broke it down. Julie opened her eyes, her ugly child's face puckered in a smile. Well, there were others.

She stretched her scrawny body languidly. Posing at the window, the drugged coke, the motel photographs—these were getting dull by now although the place in the woods was wonderful. Especially in the early morning with the mist outside, the car like an oven. That she'd keep for a while; and the violence of course. The rest would have to go. She'd think of something better next time.

Philip Harrison had never noticed the girl in his Physics class until that day—

Lazarus II

"BUT I DIED," He said.

His father looked at him without speaking. There was no expression on his face. He stood over the bed and—

Or was it the bed?

His eyes left his father's face. He looked down and it wasn't the bed. It was an experimental table. He was in the laboratory.

His eyes moved back to those of his father. He felt so heavy. So stiff. "What is it?" he asked.

And suddenly realized that the sound of his voice was different. A man didn't know the actual sound of his voice, they said. But when it changed so much, he knew. He could tell when it was no longer that voice of a man.

"Peter," his father spoke at last, "I know you'll despise me for what I've done. I despise myself already."

But Peter wasn't listening. He was trying to think. Why was he so heavy? Why couldn't he lift his head?

"Bring me a mirror," he said.

That voice. That grating, wheezing voice.

He thought he trembled.

His father didn't move.

"Peter," he said, "I want you to understand this wasn't my idea. It was your—"

"*A mirror.*"

A moment longer his father stood looking down at him. Then he turned and walked across the dark-tiled floor of the laboratory.

Peter tried to sit up. At first he couldn't. Then the room seemed to move and he knew he was sitting but there was no feeling. What was wrong? Why didn't he feel anything in his muscles? His eyes looked down.

His father took a mirror from his desk.

But Peter didn't need it. He had seen his hands.

Metal hands.

Metal arms. Metal shoulders. Metal chest. Metal trunk, metal legs, metal feet.

Metal man!

The idea made him shudder. But the metal body was still. It sat there without moving.

His body?

He tried to close his eyes. But he couldn't. They weren't his eyes. Nothing was his.

Peter was a robot.

His father came to him quickly.

"Peter, I never meant to do this," he said in a flat voice. "I don't know what came over me—it was your mother."

"Mother," said the machine hollowly.

"She said she couldn't live without you. You know how devoted she is to you."

"Devoted," he echoed.

Peter turned away. He could hear the clockwork of himself ticking in a slow, precise way. He could hear the machinery of his body with the tissue of his brain.

"You brought me back," he accused.

His brain felt mechanical too. The shock of finding his body gone and replaced with *this*. It numbed his thinking.

"I'm back," he said, trying to understand. "Why?"

Peter's father ignored his question.

He tried to get off the table, tried to raise his arms. At

first they hung down, motionless. Then, he heard a clicking in his shoulders and his arms raised up. His small glass eyes saw it and his brain knew that his arms were up.

Suddenly it swept over him. All of it.

"But I'm dead!" he cried.

He did not cry. The voice that spoke his anguish was a soft, rasping voice. An unexcited voice.

"Only your body died," his father said, trying to convince himself.

"But I'm dead!" Peter screamed.

Not screamed. The machine spoke in a quiet, orderly way. A machine-like way.

It made his mind seethe.

"Was this her idea?" he thought and was appalled to hear the hollow voice of the machine echo his thought.

His father didn't reply, standing miserably by the table, his face gaunt and lined with weariness. He was thinking that all the exhausting struggle had been for nothing. He was wondering, half in fright, if toward the end he had not been more interested in what he was doing than in why.

He watched the machine walk, clank rather, to the window, carrying his son's brain in its metal case.

Peter stared out the window. He could see the campus. See it? The red glass eyes in the skull could see, the steel skull that held his brain. The eyes registered, his brain translated. He had no eyes of his own.

"What day is it?" he asked.

"Saturday, March tenth," he heard the quiet voice of his father say, "Ten o'clock at night."

Saturday. A Saturday he'd never wanted to see. The enraging thought made him want to whirl and confront his father with vicious words. But the big steel frame clicked mechanically and eased around with a creaking sound.

"I've been working on it since Monday morning when—"

"When I killed myself," said the machine.

His father gasped, stared at him with dull eyes. He had always been so assured, so brittle, so confident. And Peter had always hated that assurance. Because he had never been assured of himself.

Himself.

It brought him back. Was this himself? Was a man only his mind? How often he had claimed that to be so. On those quiet evenings after dinner when other teachers came over and sat in the living room with him and his parents. And, while his mother sat by him, smiling and proud, he would claim that a man was his mind and nothing more. Why had she done this to him?

He felt that fettered helplessness again. The feeling of being trapped. He *was* trapped. In a great, steel-jawed snare, this body his father had made.

He had felt the same rigid terror for the past six months. The same feeling that escape was blocked in every direction. That he would never get away from the prison of his life; that chains of daily schedule hung heavy on his limbs. Often he wanted to scream.

He wanted to scream now. Louder than he ever had before. He had chosen the only remaining exit and even that was blocked. Monday morning he had slashed open his veins and the blanket of darkness had enveloped him.

Now he was back again. His body was gone. There were no veins to cut, no heart to crush or stab, no lungs to smother. Only his brain, lean and suffering. But he was back.

He stood facing the window again. Looking out over the Fort College campus. Far across he could see—the red glass lenses could see—the building where he had taught Sociological Surveys.

"Is my brain uninjured?" he asked.

Strange how the feeling seemed to abate now. A moment ago he had wanted to scream out of lungs that were no longer there. Now he felt apathetic.

"As far as I can tell," said his father.

"That's fine," Peter said, the machine said, "That's just fine."

"Peter, I want you to understand this wasn't my idea."

The machine stirred. The voice gears rubbed a little and grated but no words came. The red eyes shone out the window at the campus.

"I promised your mother," his father said, "I had to, Peter. She was hysterical. She—there was no other way."

"And besides, it was a most interesting experiment," said the voice of the machine, his son.

Silence.

"Peter Dearfield," said Peter, said the turning, twinkling gears in the steel throat, "Peter Dearfield is resurrected!" He turned to look at his father. He knew in his mind that a living heart would have been beating heavily, but the little wheels turned methodically. The hands did not tremble, but hung in polished muteness at his steel sides. There was no heart to beat. And no breath to catch, for the body was not alive but a machine.

"Take out my brain," Peter said.

His father began to put on his vest; his tired fingers buttoned it slowly.

"You can't leave me like this."

"Peter, I—I must."

"For the experiment?"

"For your mother."

"You hate her and you hate me!"

His father shook his head.

"Then I'll do it myself," intoned the machine.

The steel hands reached up.

"You can't," said his father, "You can't harm yourself."

"Damn you!"

• • •

No outraged cry followed. Did his father know that, in his mind, Peter was screaming? The sound of his voice was mild. It could not enrage. Could the well-modulated requests of a machine be heeded?

The legs moved heavily. The clanking body moved toward Doctor Dearfield. He raised his eyes.

"And have you taken out the ability to kill?" asked the machine.

The old man looked at the machine standing before him. The machine that was his only son.

"No," he said, wearily, "You can kill me."

The machine seemed to falter. Gears struck teeth, reversed themselves.

"Experiment successful," said the flat voice, "You've made your own son into a machine."

His father stood there with a tired look on his face.

"Have I?" he said.

Peter turned from his father with a clicking of gears not trying to speak, and moved over to the wall mirror.

"Don't you want to see your mother?" asked his father.

Peter made no answer. He stopped before the mirror and the little glass eyes looked at themselves.

He wanted to tear the brain out of its steel container and hurl it away.

No mouth. No nose. A gleaming red eye on the right and a gleaming red eye on the left.

A head like a bucket. All with little rivets like tiny bumps on his new metal skin.

"And you did all this for *her*," he said.

He turned on well-oiled wheels. The red eyes did not show the hate behind them. "Liar," said the machine. "You did it for yourself—for the pleasure of experimenting."

If only he could rush at his father. If only he could stamp and flail his arms wildly and scream until the laboratory echoed with the screams.

But how could he? His voice went on as before. A whisper, a turning of oiled wheels, spinning like gears in a clock.

His brain turned and turned.

"You thought you'd make her happy, didn't you?" Peter said, "You thought she'd run to me and embrace me. You thought she'd kiss my soft, warm skin. You thought she'd look into my blue eyes and tell me how handsome I—"

"Peter this will do no—"

"—how *handsome* I am. Kiss me on the mouth."

He stepped toward the old doctor on slow, steel legs. His eyes flickered in the fluorescent light of the small laboratory.

"Will she kiss my mouth?" Peter asked, "You haven't given me one."

His father's skin was ashen. His hands trembled.

"You did it for yourself," said the machine, "You never cared about her—or about me."

"Your mother is waiting," his father said, quietly putting on his coat.

"I'm not going."

"Peter, she's waiting."

The thought made Peter's mind swell up in anguish. It ached and throbbed in its hard, metal casing. Mother, mother, how can I look at you now? After what I've done. Even though these aren't my own eyes, how can I look at you now?

"She mustn't see me like this," insisted the machine.

"She's waiting to see you."

"*No!*"

Not a cry, but a mannerly turning of wheels.

"She *wants* you Peter."

He felt helpless again. Trapped. He was back. His mother was waiting for him.

The legs moved him. His father opened the door and he went out to his mother.

● ● ●

She stood up suddenly from the bench, one hand clutching her throat, the other holding her dark, leather handbag. Her eyes were fastened on the robot. The color left her cheeks.

"Peter," she said. Only a whisper.

He looked at her. At her grey hair, her soft skin, the gentle mouth and eyes. The stooped form, the old overcoat she'd worn so many years because she'd insisted that he take her extra money and buy clothes for himself.

He looked at his mother who wanted him so much she would not let even death take him from her.

"Mother," said the machine, forgetting for a moment.

Then he saw the twitching in her face. And he realized what he was.

He stood motionless; her eyes fled to his father standing beside him. And Peter saw what her eyes said.

They said—why like *this?*

He wanted to turn and run. He wanted to die. When he had killed himself the despair was a quiet one, a despair of hopelessness. It had not been this brain-bursting agony. His life had ebbed away silently and peacefully. Now he wanted to destroy it in an instant, violently.

"Peter," she said.

But she did not smother him with kisses. How could she, his brain tortured. Would anyone *kiss* a suit of armor?

How long would she stand there, staring at him? He felt the rage mounting in his mind.

"Aren't you satisfied?" he said.

But something went wrong inside him and his words were jumbled into a mechanical croaking. He saw his mother's lips tremble. Again she looked at his father. Then back at the machine. Guiltily.

"How do you—feel, Peter?"

There was no hollow laughter even though his brain

wanted to send out hollow laughter. Instead the gears began to grind and he heard nothing but the friction of gnashing teeth. He saw his mother try to smile, then fail to conceal her look of sick horror.

"Peter," she wailed, slumping to the floor.

"I'll tear it apart," he heard his father saying huskily, "I'll destroy it."

For Peter there was an upsurge of hope.

But then his mother stopped trembling. She pulled away from her husband's grip.

"No," she said and Peter heard the granite-like resolve in her voice, the strength he knew so well.

"I'll be all right in a minute," she said.

She walked straight toward him, smiling.

"It's all right, Peter," she said.

"Am I handsome, Mother?" he asked.

"Peter, you—"

"Don't you want to kiss me, mother?" asked the machine.

He saw her throat move. He saw tears on her cheeks. Then she leaned forward. He could not feel her lips press against the cool steel. He only heard it, a slight thumping against the metal skin.

"Peter," she said, "Forgive us for what we've done."

All he could think was—

Can a machine forgive?

They took him out the back doorway of the Physical Sciences Center. They tried to hustle him to the car. But halfway down the walk Peter saw everything spin around and there was a stabbing in his brain as the mass of his new body crashed backward on the cement.

His mother gasped and looked down at him in fright.

His father bent over and Peter saw his fingers working on the right knee joint. His voice was muffled as he worked.

"How does your brain feel?"

He didn't answer. The red eyes glinted.

"Peter," his father said urgently.

He didn't answer. He stared at the dark trees that lined Eleventh Street.

"You can get up now," his father said.

"No."

"Peter, not here."

"I'm not getting up," the machine said.

"Peter, please," his mother begged.

"No, I can't, mother, I can't."

Spoken like a hideous metal monster.

"Peter, you can't stay *there*."

The memory of all the years before stopped him. He would not get up.

"Let them find me," he said, "Maybe *they'll* destroy me."

His father looked around with worried eyes. And, suddenly, Peter realized that no one knew of this but his parents. If the board found out, his father would be pilloried. He found the idea pleased him.

But his wired reflexes were too slow to stop his father from placing hands on his chest and pulling open a small hinged door.

Before he could swing one of his clumsy arms, his father flicked his mechanism and, abruptly, the arm stopped as the connection between his will and the machinery was broken.

Doctor Dearfield pushed a button and the robot stood and walked stiffly to the car. He followed behind, his frail chest laboring for breath. He kept thinking what a horrible mistake he had made to listen to his wife. Why did he always let her alter his decisions?

Why had he allowed her to control their son when he lived? Why had he let her convince him to bring their son back when he had made a last, desperate attempt to escape?

His robot son sat in the back seat stiffly. Doctor Dearfield slid into the car beside his wife.

"Now he's perfect," he said, "Now you can lead him around as you please. A pity he wasn't so agreeable in life. Almost as pliable, almost as machine-like. But not quite. He didn't do *everything* you wanted him to."

She looked at her husband with surprise, glancing back at the robot as if afraid it might hear. It was her son's mind. And she had said a man was his mind.

The sweet, unsullied mind of her son! The mind she had always protected and sheltered from the ugly taint of worldliness. He was her life. She did not feel guilty for having him brought back. If only he weren't so. . . .

"Are you satisfied, Ruth?" asked her husband, "Oh, don't worry; he can't hear me."

But he could. He sat there and listened. Peter's brain heard.

"You're not answering me," said Doctor Dearfield, starting the motor.

"I don't want to talk about it."

"You have to talk about it," he said, "What have you planned for him now? You always made it a point to live his life before."

"Stop it, John."

"No, you've broken my silence, Ruth. I must have been insane to listen to you. Insane to let myself get interested in such a—hideous project. To bring you back your dead son."

"Is it hideous that I love my son and want him with me?"

"It's hideous that you defy his last desire on Earth! To be dead and free of you and at peace at last."

"Free of me, free of me," she screamed angrily, "Am I such a monster?"

"No," he said quietly, "But, with my help, you've certainly made our son a monster." She did not speak. Peter saw her lips draw into a thin line.

"What will he do now?" asked her husband, "Go back to his classes? Teach sociology?"

"I don't know," she murmured.

"No, of course you don't. All you ever worried about was his being near you."

Doctor Dearfield turned the corner. He started up College Avenue.

"I know," he said, "We'll use him for an ashtray."

"John, stop it!"

She slumped forward and Peter heard her sobbing. He watched his mother with the red glass eyes of the machine he lived in.

"Did you—h-have to make him so—so—"

"So ugly?"

"I—"

"Ruth, I *told* you what he'd look like. You just glossed over my words. All you could think of was getting your claws into him again."

"I didn't, I didn't," she sobbed.

"Did you ever respect a single one of his wishes?" her husband asked. *"Did* you? When he wanted to write, would you let him? No! You scoffed. Be practical, darling, you said. It's a pretty thought but we must be practical. Your father will get you a nice position with the college."

She shook her head silently.

"When he wanted to go to New York to live, would you let him? When he wanted to marry Elizabeth, would you let him?"

The angry words of his father faded as Peter looked out at the dark campus on his right. He was thinking, dreaming, of a pretty, dark-haired girl in his class. Remembering the day she'd spoken to him. Of the walks, the concerts, the soft, exciting kisses, the tender, shy caresses.

If only he could sob, cry out.

But a machine could not cry and it had no heart to break.

"Year after year," his father's voice fluttered back into hearing, "Turning him into a machine even then."

And Peter's mind pictured the long, elliptical walk

around the campus. The walk he had so many times trudged to and from classes, briefcase gripped firmly in his hand. The dark gray hat on his balding head, balding at twenty-eight! The heavy overcoat in winter, the gray tweed suit in fall and spring. The lined seersucker during the hot months when he taught summer session.

Nothing but depressing days that stretched on endlessly.

Until he had ended them.

"He's still my son," he heard his mother saying.

"Is he?" mocked his father.

"It's still his mind, and a man's mind is everything."

"What about his body?" her husband persisted, "What about his hands? They are just two pronged claws like *hooks*. Will you hold his hands as you used to? Those riveted metal arms—would you let him put those arms around you and embrace you?"

"John *please*—"

"What will you do with him? Put him in a closet? Hide him when guests come? What will you—"

"I don't want to *talk* about it!"

"You *must* talk about it! What about his face? Can you kiss that face?"

She trembled and, suddenly, her husband drove the car to the curb and stopped it with a jerk. He grabbed her shoulder and turned her forcibly around.

"*Look at him!* Can you kiss that metal face? Is it your son, is *that* your son?"

She could not look. And it was the final blow at Peter's brain. He knew that she had not loved his mind, his personality, his character at all. It was the living person she had doted upon, the body *she* could direct, the hands *she* could hold—the responses *she* could control.

"You never loved him," his father said cruelly. "You *possessed* him. You *destroyed* him."

"Destroyed!" she moaned in anguish.

And then they both spun around in horror. Because the machine had said, "Yes. Destroyed."

His father was staring at him.

"I thought—" he said, thinly.

"I am now, in objective form, what I have always been," said the robot. "A well-controlled machine."

The throat gears made sound.

"Mother, take home your little boy," said the machine.

But Doctor Dearfield had already turned the car around and was heading back.

Big Surprise

OLD MR. HAWKINS used to stand by his picket fence and call to the little boys when they were coming home from school.

"Lad!" he would call. "Come here, lad!"

Most of the little boys were afraid to go near him, so they laughed and made fun of him in voices that shook. Then they ran away and told their friends how brave they'd been. But once in a while a boy would go up to Mr. Hawkins when he called, and Mr. Hawkins would make his strange request.

That was how the verse got started:

> Dig me a hole, he says,
> Winking his eyes,
> And you will find
> A big surprise.

No one knew how long they'd heard the children chanting it. Sometimes the parents seemed to recall having heard it years ago.

Once a little boy started to dig the hole but he got tired after a while and he didn't find any big surprise. He was the only one who had ever tried—

One day Ernie Willaker was coming home from school with two of his friends. They walked on the other side of the street when they saw Mr. Hawkins in his front yard standing by the picket fence.

"Lad!" they heard him call. "Come here, lad!"

"He means you, Ernie," teased one of the boys.

"He does not," said Ernie.

Mr. Hawkins pointed a finger at Ernie. "Come here, lad!" he called.

Ernie glanced nervously at his friends.

"Go on," said one of them. "What're ya scared of?"

"Who's scared?" said Ernie. "My ma says I have to come home right after school is all."

"Yella," said his other friend. "You're scared of old man Hawkins."

"Who's scared!"

"Go *on*, then."

"Lad!" called Mr. Hawkins. "Come here, lad."

"Well." Ernie hesitated. "Don't *go* nowhere," he said.

"We won't. We'll stick around."

"Well—" Ernie braced himself and crossed the street, trying to look casual. He shifted his books to his left hand and brushed back his hair with his right. *Dig me a hole, he says,* muttered in his brain.

Ernie stepped up to the picket fence. "Yes, sir?" he asked.

"Come closer, lad," the old man said, his dark eyes shining.

Ernie took a forward step.

"Now you aren't afraid of Mister Hawkins, are you?" said the old man winking.

"No, sir," Ernie said.

"Good," said the old man. "Now listen, lad. How would you like a big surprise?"

Ernie glanced across his shoulder. His friends were still there. He grinned at them. Suddenly he gasped as a gaunt hand clamped over his right arm. "Hey, leggo!" Ernie cried out.

"Take it easy, lad," soothed Mr. Hawkins. "No one's going to hurt you."

Ernie tugged. Tears sprang into his eyes as the old man drew him closer. From the corner of an eye Ernie saw his two friends running down the street.

"L-leggo," Ernie sobbed.

"Shortly," said the old man. "Now then, would you like a big surprise?"

"N-no, thanks, mister."

"Sure you would," said Mr. Hawkins. Ernie smelled his breath and tried to pull away, but Mr. Hawkins's grip was like iron.

"You know where Mr. Miller's field is?" asked Mr. Hawkins.

"Y-yeah."

"You know where the big oak tree is?"

"Yeah. Yeah, I know."

"You go to the oak tree in Mr. Miller's field and face toward the church steeple. You understand?"

"Y-y-yeah."

The old man drew him closer. "You stand there and you walk ten paces. You understand? Ten paces."

"Yeah—"

"You walk ten paces and you dig down ten feet. *How many feet?*" He prodded Ernie's chest with a bony finger.

"T-ten," said Ernie.

"That's it," said the old man. "Face the steeple, walk ten paces, dig ten feet—and there you'll find a big surprise." He winked at Ernie. "Will you do it, lad?"

"I—yeah, sure. *Sure.*"

Mr. Hawkins let go and Ernie jumped away. His arm felt completely numb.

"Don't forget, now," the old man said.

Ernie whirled and ran down the street as fast as he could. He found his friends waiting at the corner.

"Did he try and murder you?" one of them whispered.

"Nanh," said Ernie, "He ain't so m-much."

"What'd he want?"

"What d'ya s'pose?"

They started down the street, all chanting it.

> Dig me a hole, he said,
> Winking his eyes,
> And you will find
> A big surprise.

Every afternoon they went to Mr. Miller's field and sat under the big oak tree.

"You think there's somethin' down there really?"

"Nanh."

"What if there *was* though?"

"What?"

"Gold, maybe."

They talked about it every day, and every day they faced the steeple and walked ten paces. They stood on the spot and scuffed the earth with the tips of their sneakers.

"You s'pose there's gold down there really?"

"Why should he tell us?"

"Yeah, why not dig it up himself?"

"Because he's too old, stupid."

"Yeah? Well, if there's gold down there we split in three ways."

They became more and more curious. At night they dreamed about gold. They wrote *gold* in their schoolbooks. They thought about all the things they could buy with gold. They started walking past Mr. Hawkins's house to see if he'd call them again and they could asked him if it was gold. But he never called them.

Then, one day, they were coming home from school and they saw Mr. Hawkins talking to another boy.

"He told us *we* could have the gold!" said Ernie.

"Yeah!" they stormed angrily. "Let's go!"

They ran to Ernie's house and Ernie went down to the cellar and got shovels. They ran up the street, over lots, across the dump, and into Mr. Miller's field. They stood under the oak tree, faced the steeple, and paced ten times.

"Dig," said Ernie.

Their shovels sank into the black earth. They dug without speaking, breath whistling through their nostrils. When the hole was about three feet deep, they rested.

"You think there's gold down there really?"

"I don't know but we're gonna find out before that other kid does."

"Yeah!"

"Hey, how we gonna get out if we dig ten feet?" one of them said.

"We'll cut out steps," said Ernie.

They started digging again. For over an hour they shoveled out the cool, wormy earth and piled it high around the hole. It stained their clothes and their skin. When the hole was over their heads one of them went to get a pail and a rope. Ernie and the other boy kept digging and throwing the earth out of the hole. After a while the dirt rained back on their heads and they stopped. They sat on the damp earth wearily, waiting for the other boy to come back. Their hands and arms were brown with earth.

"How far're we down?" wondered the boy.

"Six feet," estimated Ernie.

The other boy came back and they started working again. They kept digging and digging until their bones ached.

"Aaah, the heck with it," said the boy who was pulling up the pail. "There's ain't nothin' down there."

"He said ten feet," Ernie insisted.

"Well, I'm quittin'," said the boy.

"You're yella!"

"Tough," said the boy.

Ernie turned to the boy beside him. "You'll have to pull the dirt up," he said.

"Oh—okay," muttered the boy.

Ernie kept digging. When he looked up now, it seemed as if the sides of the hole were shaking and it was all going to cave in on him. He was trembling with fatigue.

"Come on," the other boy finally called down. "There ain't nothin' down there. You dug ten feet."

"Not yet," gasped Ernie.

"How deep ya goin', *China?*"

Ernie leaned against the side of the hole and gritted his teeth. A fat worm crawled out of the earth and tumbled to the bottom of the hole.

"I'm goin' home," said the other boy. "I'll catch it if I'm late for supper."

"You're yella too," said Ernie miserably.

"Aaaah—*tough.*"

Ernie twisted his shoulders painfully. "Well, the gold is all mine," he called up.

"There ain't no gold," said the other boy.

"Tie the rope to something so I can get out when I find *the gold,*" said Ernie.

The boy snickered. He tied the rope to a bush and let it dangle down into the hole. Ernie looked up and saw the crooked rectangle of darkening sky. The boy's face appeared, looking down.

"You better not get stuck down there," he said.

"I ain't gettin' stuck." Ernie looked down angrily and drove the shovel into the ground. He could feel his friend's eyes on his back.

"Ain't you scared?" asked the other boy.

"What of?" snapped Ernie without looking up.

"I dunno," said the boy.

Ernie dug.

"Well," said the boy. "I'll see ya."

Ernie grunted. He heard the boy's footsteps move away. He looked around the hole and a faint whimper sounded in his throat. He felt cold.

"Well, I ain't leavin'," he mumbled. The gold was his.

He wasn't going to leave it for the other kid.

He dug furiously, piling the dirt on the other side of the hole. It kept getting darker.

"A little more," he told himself, gasping. "Then I'm goin' home with the gold."

He stepped hard on the shovel and there was a hollow sound beneath him. Ernie felt a shudder running up his back. He forced himself to keep on digging. Will I give *them* the horse laugh, he thought. Will I give *them*—

He had uncovered part of a box—a long box. He stood there looking down at the wood and shivering. *And you will find—*

Quivering, Ernie stood on top of the box and stamped on it. A deeply hollow sound struck his ears. He dug away more earth and his shovel scraped on the ancient wood. He couldn't uncover the entire box—it was too long.

Then he saw that the box had a two-part cover and there was a clasp on each part.

Ernie clenched his teeth and struck the clasp with the edge of his shovel. Half of the cover opened.

Ernie screamed. He fell back against the earth wall and stared in voiceless horror at the man who was sitting up.

"Surprise!" said Mr. Hawkins.

Crickets

AFTER SUPPER, they walked down to the lake and looked at its moon-reflecting surface.

"Pretty, isn't it?" she said.

"Mmm-hmm."

"It's been a nice vacation."

"Yes, it has," he said.

Behind them, the screen door on the hotel porch opened and shut. Someone started down the gravel path toward the lake. Jean glanced over her shoulder.

"Who is it?" asked Hal without turning.

"That man we saw in the dining room," she said. In a few moments, the man stood nearby on the shoreline. He didn't speak or look at them. He stared across the lake at the distant woods.

"Should we talk to him?" whispered Jean.

"I don't know," he whispered back.

They looked at the lake again and Hal's arm slipped around her waist.

Suddenly the man asked:

"Do you hear them?"

"Sir?" said Hal.

The small man turned and looked at them. His eyes appeared to glitter in the moonlight.

"I asked if you heard them," he said.

There was a brief pause before Hal asked, "Who?"

"The crickets."

The two of them stood quietly. Then Jean cleared

her throat. "Yes, they're nice," she said.

"*Nice?*" The man turned away. After a moment, he turned back and came walking over to them.

"My name is John Morgan," he said.

"Hal and Jean Galloway," Hal told him and then there was an awkward silence.

"It's a lovely night," Jean offered.

"It would be if it weren't for them," said Mr. Morgan. "The crickets."

"Why don't you like them?" asked Jean.

Mr. Morgan seemed to listen for a moment, his face rigid. His gaunt throat moved. Then he forced a smile.

"Allow me the pleasure of buying you a glass of wine," he said.

"Well—" Hal began.

"Please." There was a sudden urgency in Mr. Morgan's voice.

The dining hall was like a vast shadowy cavern. The only light came from the small lamp on their table which cast up formless shadows of them on the walls.

"Your health," said Mr. Morgan, raising his glass. The wine was dry and tart. It trickled in chilly drops down Jean's throat, making her shiver.

"So what about the crickets?" asked Hal.

Mr. Morgan put his glass down.

"I don't know whether I should tell you," he said. He looked at them carefully. Jean felt restive under his surveillance and reached out to take a sip from her glass.

Suddenly, with a movement so brusque that it made her hand twitch and spill some wine, Mr. Morgan drew a small, black notebook from his coat pocket. He put it on the table carefully.

"There," he said.

"What is it?" asked Hal.

"A code book," said Mr. Morgan.

They watched him pour more wine into his glass,

then set down the bottle and the bottle's shadow on the table cloth. He picked up the glass and rolled its stem between his fingers.

"It's the code of the crickets," he said.

Jean shuddered. She didn't know why. There was nothing terrible about the words. It was the way Mr. Morgan had spoken them.

Mr. Morgan leaned forward, his eyes glowing in the lamplight.

"Listen," he said. "They aren't just making indiscriminate noises when they rub their wings together." He paused. *"They're sending messages,"* he said.

Jean felt as if she were a block of wood. The room seemed to shift balance around her, everything leaning toward her.

"Why are you telling us?" asked Hal.

"Because now I'm sure," said Mr. Morgan. He leaned in close. "Have you ever really listened to the crickets?" he asked, "I mean really? If you had you'd have heard a rhythm to their noises. A pace—a definite beat.

"I've listened," he said. "For seven years I've listened. And the more I listened the more I became convinced that their noise was a code; that they were sending messages in the night.

"Then—about a week ago—I suddenly heard the pattern. It's like a Morse code only, of course, the sounds are different."

Mr. Morgan stopped talking and looked at his black notebook.

"And there it is," he said. "After seven years of work, here it is. I've deciphered it."

His throat worked convulsively as he picked up his glass and emptied it with a swallow.

"Well—what are they saying?" Hal asked, awkwardly.

Mr. Morgan looked at him.

"Names," he said. "Look, I'll show you."

He reached into one of his pockets and drew out a stubby pencil. Tearing a blank page from his notebook, he started to write on it, muttering to himself.

"Pulse, pulse—silence—pulse, pulsepulse—silence—pulse—silence—"

Hal and Jean looked at each other. Hal tried to smile but couldn't. Then they were looking back at the small man bent over the table, listening to the crickets and writing.

Mr. Morgan put down the pencil. "It will give you some idea," he said, holding out the sheet to them. They looked at it.

MARIE CADMAN, it read. JOHN JOSEPH ALSTER. SAMUEL—

"You see," said Mr. Morgan, "Names."

"Whose?" Jean had to ask it even though she didn't want to.

Mr. Morgan held the book in a clenching hand.

"The names of the dead," he answered.

Later that night, Jean climbed into bed with Hal and pressed close to him. "I'm cold," she murmured.

"You're scared."

"Aren't you?"

"Well," he said, "if I am, it isn't in the way you think."

"How's that?"

"I don't believe what he said. But he might be a dangerous man. That's what I'm afraid of."

"Where'd he get those names?"

"Maybe they're friends of his," he said. "Maybe he got them from tombstones. He might have just made them up." He grunted softly. "But I don't think the crickets told him," he said.

Jean snuggled against him.

"I'm glad you told him we were tired," she said. "I

don't think I could have taken much more."

"Honey," he said, "Here that nice little man was giving us the lowdown on crickets and you disparage him."

"Hal," she said, "I'll never be able to enjoy crickets for the rest of my life."

They lay close to each other and slept. And, outside in the still darkness, crickets rubbed their wings together until morning came.

Mr. Morgan came rapidly across the dining room and sat down at their table.

"I've been looking for you all day," he said. "You've got to help me."

Hal's mouth tightened. "Help you how?" he asked, putting down his fork.

"They know I'm on to them," said Mr. Morgan. "They're after me."

"Who, the crickets?" Hal asked, jadedly.

"I don't know," said Mr. Morgan, "Either them or—"

Jean held her knife and fork with rigid fingers. For some reason, she felt a chill creeping up her legs.

"Mr. Morgan." Hal was trying to sound patient.

"Understand me," Mr. Morgan pleaded. "The crickets are under the command of the dead. The dead send out these messages."

"Why?"

"They're compiling a list of all their names," said Mr. Morgan. "They keep sending the names through the crickets to let the others know."

"Why?" repeated Hal.

Mr. Morgan's hands trembled. "I don't know, I don't know," he said. "Maybe when there are enough names, when enough of them are ready, they'll—" His throat moved convulsively. *"They'll come back,"* he said.

After a moment, Hal asked, "What makes you think

you're in any danger?"

"Because while I was writing down more names last night," said Mr. Morgan, *"they spelled out my name."*

Hal broke the heavy silence.

"What can we do?" he asked in a voice that bordered on uneasiness.

"Stay with me," said Mr. Morgan, "so they can't get me."

Jean looked nervously at Hal.

"I won't bother you," said Mr. Morgan, "I won't even sit here, I'll sit across the room. Just so I can see you."

He stood up quickly and took out his notebook.

"Will you watch this?" he asked.

Before they could say another word, he left their table and walked across the dining room, weaving in and out among the white-clothed tables. About fifty feet from them, he sat down, facing them. They saw him reach forward and turn on the table lamp.

"What do we do now?" asked Jean.

"We'll stay here a little while," said Hal, "Nurse the bottle along. When it's empty, we'll go to bed."

"Do we have to stay?"

"Honey, who knows what's going on in that mind of his? I don't want to take any chances."

Jean closed her eyes and exhaled wearily. "What a way to polish off a vacation," she said.

Hal reached over and picked up the notebook. As he did, he became conscious of the crickets rasping outside. He flipped through the pages. They were arranged in alphabetical order, on each page three letters with their pulse equivalents.

"He's watching us," said Jean.

"Forget him."

Jean leaned over and looked at the notebook with him. Her eyes moved over the arrangements of dots and dashes.

"You think there's anything to this?" she asked.

"Let's hope not," said Hal.

He tried to listen to the crickets' noise and find some point of comparison with the notes. He couldn't. After several minutes, he shut the book.

When the wine bottle was empty, Hal stood. "Beddy-bye," he said.

Before Jean was on her feet, Mr. Morgan was halfway to their table. "You're leaving?" he asked.

"Mr. Morgan, it's almost eleven," Hal said. "We're tired. I'm sorry but we have to go to bed."

The small man stood wordless, looking from one to the other with pleading, hopeless eyes. He seemed about to speak, then his narrow shoulders slumped and his gaze dropped to the floor. They heard him swallowing.

"You'll take care of the book?" he asked.

"Don't you want it?"

"No." Mr. Morgan turned away. After a few paces, he stopped and glanced back across his shoulder. "Could you leave your door open so I can—call?"

"All right, Mr. Morgan," he said.

A faint smile twitched Mr. Morgan's lips.

"Thank you," he said and walked away.

It was after four when the screaming woke them. Hal felt Jean's fingers clutching at his arm as they both jolted to a sitting position, staring into the darkness.

"What is it?" gasped Jean.

"I don't know." Hal threw off the covers and dropped his feet to the floor.

"Don't leave me!" said Jean.

"Come on then!"

The hall had a dim bulb burning overhead. Hal sprinted over the floorboards toward Mr. Morgan's room. The door to it was closed although it had been left open before. Hal banged his fist on it. "Mr. Morgan!" he called.

Inside the room, there was a sudden, rustling,

crackling sound—like that of a million, wildly shaken tambourines. The noise made Hal's hand jerk back convulsively from the door knob.

"What's *that?*" Jean asked in a terrified whisper.

He didn't answer. They stood immobile, not knowing what to do. Then, inside, the noise stopped. Hal took a deep breath and pushed open the door.

The scream gagged in Jean's throat.

Lying in a pool of blood-splotched moonlight was Mr. Morgan, his skin raked open as if by a thousand tiny razor blades. There was a gaping hole in the window screen.

Jean stood paralyzed, a fist pressed against her mouth while Hal moved to Mr. Morgan's side. He knelt down beside the motionless man and felt at Mr. Morgan's chest where the pajama top had been sliced to ribbons. The faintest of heartbeats pulsed beneath his trembling fingers.

Mr. Morgan opened his eyes. Wide, staring eyes that recognized nothing, that looked right through Hal.

"P-H-I-L-I-P   M-A-X-W-E-L-L." Mr. Morgan spelled out the name in a bubbling voice.

"M-A-R-Y G-A-B-R-I-E-L," spelled Mr. Morgan, eyes stark and glazed.

His chest lurched once. His eyes widened.

"J-O-H-N M-O-R-G-A-N," he spelled.

Then his eyes began focusing on Hal. There was a terrible rattling in his throat. As though the sounds were wrenched from him one by one by a power beyond his own, he spoke again.

"H A R O L D G-A-L-L-O-W-A-Y," he spelled, "J-E-A-N G-A-L-L-O-W-A-Y."

Then they were alone with a dead man. And outside in the night, a million crickets rustled their wings together. And waited.

Mute

THE MAN IN the dark raincoat arrived in German Corners at two-thirty that Friday afternoon. He walked across the bus station to a counter behind which a plump, grey-haired woman was polishing glasses.

"Please," he said, "Where might I find authority?"

The woman peered through rimless glasses at him. She saw a man in his late thirties, a tall, good-looking man.

"Authority?" she asked.

"Yes—how do you say it? The constable? The—?"

"Sheriff?"

"Ah." The man smiled. "Of course. The sheriff. Where might I find him?"

After being directed, he walked out of the building into the overcast day. The threat of rain had been constant since he'd woken up that morning as the bus was pulling over the mountains into Casca Valley. The man drew up his collar, then slid both hands into the pockets of his raincoat and started briskly down Main Street.

Really, he felt tremendously guilty for not having come sooner; but there was so much to do, so many problems to overcome with his own two children. Even knowing that something was wrong with Holger and Fanny, he'd been unable to get away from Germany until now—almost a year since they'd last heard from the Nielsens. It was a shame that Holger had chosen such an out of the way place for his corner of the four-sided experiment.

Professor Werner walked more quickly, anxious to find out what had happened to the Nielsens and their son. Their progress with the boy had been phenomenal—really an inspiration to them all. Although, Werner felt, deep within himself, that something terrible had happened he hoped they were all alive and well. Yet, if they were, how to account for the long silence?

Werner shook his head worriedly. Could it have been the town? Elkenberg had been compelled to move several times in order to avoid the endless prying— sometimes innocent, more often malicious—into *his* work. Something similar might have happened to Nielsen. The workings of the small town composite mind could, sometimes, be a terrible thing.

The sheriff's office was in the middle of the next block. Werner strode more quickly along the narrow sidewalk, then pushed open the door and entered the large, warm heated room.

"Yes?" the sheriff asked, looking up from his desk.

"I have come to inquire about a family," Werner said, "The name of Nielsen."

Sheriff Harry Wheeler looked blankly at the tall man.

Cora was pressing Paul's trousers when the call came. Setting the iron on its stand, she walked across the kitchen and lifted the receiver from the wall telephone.

"Yes?" she said.

"Cora, it's me."

Her face tightened. "Is something wrong, Harry?"

He was silent.

"Harry?"

"The one from Germany is here."

Cora stood motionless, staring at the calendar on the wall, the numbers blurred before her eyes.

"Cora, did you hear me?"

She swallowed dryly. "Yes."

"I—I have to bring him out to the house," he said.

She closed her eyes.

"I know," she murmured and hung up.

Turning, she walked slowly to the window. It's going to rain, she thought. Nature was setting the scene well.

Abruptly, her eyes shut, her fingers drew in tautly, the nails digging at her palms.

"No." It was almost a gasp. "No."

After a few moments she opened her tear-glistening eyes and looked out fixedly at the road. She stood there numbly, thinking of the day the boy had come to her.

If the house hadn't burned in the middle of the night there might have been a chance. It was twenty-one miles from German Corners but the state highway ran fifteen of them and the last six—the six miles of dirt road that led north into the wood-sloped hills—might have been navigated had there been more time.

As it happened, the house was a night-lashing sheet of flame before Bernhard Klaus saw it.

Klaus and his family lived some five miles away on Skytouch Hill. He had gotten out of bed around one-thirty to get a drink of water. The window of the bathroom faced north and that was why, entering, Klaus saw the tiny flaring blaze out in the darkness.

"*Gott'n'immel!*" he slung startled words together and was out of the room before he'd finished. He thumped heavily down the carpeted steps, then, feeling at the wall for guidance, hurried for the living room.

"Fire at Nielsen house!" he gasped after agitated cranking had roused the night operator from her nap.

The hour, the remoteness, and one more thing doomed the house. German Corners had no official fire brigade. The security of its brick and timbered dwellings depended on voluntary effort. In the town itself this posed no serious problem. It was different with those houses in the outlying areas.

By the time Sheriff Harry Wheeler had gathered five men and driven them to the fire on the ancient truck, the house was lost. While four of the six men pumped futile streams of water into the leaping, crackling inferno, Sheriff Wheeler and his deputy, Max Ederman, circuited the house.

There was no way in. They stood in back, raised arms warding off the singeing buffet of heat, grimacing at the blaze.

"They're done for!" Ederman yelled above the windswept roar.

Sheriff Wheeler looked sick. "The *boy*," he said but Ederman didn't hear.

Only a waterfall could have doused the burning of the old house. All the six men could do was prevent ignition of the woods that fringed the clearing. Their silent figures prowled the edges of the glowing aura, stamping out sparks, hosing out the occasional flare of bushes and tree foliage.

They found the boy just as the eastern hill peaks were being edged with grey morning.

Sheriff Wheeler was trying to get close enough to see into one of the side windows when he heard a shout. Turning, he ran toward the thick woods that sloped downward a few dozen yards behind the house. Before he'd reached the underbrush, Tom Poulter emerged from them, his thin frame staggering beneath the weight of Paal Nielsen.

"Where'd you find him?" Wheeler asked, grabbing the boy's legs to ease weight from the older man's back.

"Down the hill," Poulter gasped. "Lyin' on the ground."

"Is he burned?"

"Don't look it. His pajamas ain't touched."

"Give him here," the sheriff said. He shifted Paal

into his own strong arms and found two large, green-pupiled eyes staring blankly at him.

"You're awake," he said, surprised.

The boy kept staring at him without making a sound.

"You all right, son?" Wheeler asked. It might have been a statue he held, Paal's body was so inert, his expression so dumbly static.

"Let's get a blanket on him," the sheriff muttered aside and started for the truck. As he walked he noticed how the boy stared at the burning house now, a look of masklike rigidity on his face.

"Shock," murmured Poulter and the sheriff nodded grimly.

They tried to put him down on the cab seat, a blanket over him, but he kept sitting up, never speaking. The coffee Wheeler tried to give him dribbled from his lips and across his chin. The two men stood beside the truck while Paal stared through the windshield at the burning house.

"Bad off," said Poulter, "Can't talk, cry nor nothin'."

"He isn't burned," Wheeler said, perplexed. "How'd he get out of the house without getting burned?"

"Maybe his folks got out too," said Poulter.

"Where are they then?"

The older man shook his head. "Dunno, Harry."

"Well, I better take him home to Cora," the sheriff said, "Can't leave him sitting out here."

"Think I'd better go with you," Poulter said, "I have t'get the mail sorted for delivery."

"All right."

Wheeler told the other four men he'd bring back food and replacements in an hour or so. Then Poulter and he climbed into the cab beside Paal and he jabbed his boot toe on the starter. The engine coughed spasmodically, groaned over, then caught. The sheriff raced it until it was warm, then eased it into gear. The truck rolled off slowly down the dirt road that led to the highway.

Until the burning house was no longer visible, Paal stared out the back window, face still immobile. Then, slowly, he turned, the blanket slipping off his thin shoulders. Tom Poulter put it back over him.

"Warm enough?" he asked.

The silent boy looked at Poulter as if he'd never heard a human voice in his life.

As soon as she heard the truck turn off the road, Cora Wheeler's quick right hand moved along the stove-front switches. Before her husband's bootfalls sounded on the back porch steps, the bacon lay neatly in strips across the frying pan, white moons of pancake batter were browning on the griddle, and the already brewed coffee was heating.

"*Harry.*"

There was a sound of pitying distress in her voice as she saw the boy in his arms. She hurried across the kitchen.

"Let's get him to bed," Wheeler said, "I think maybe he's in shock."

The slender woman moved up the stairs on hurried feet, threw open the door of what had been David's room, and moved to the bed. When Wheeler passed through the doorway she had the covers peeled back and was plugging in an electric blanket.

"Is he hurt?" she asked.

"No." He put Paal down on the bed.

"Poor darling," she murmured, tucking in the bedclothes around the boy's frail body. "Poor little darling." She stroked back the soft blonde hair from his forehead and smiled down at him.

"There now, go to sleep, dear. It's all right. Go to sleep."

Wheeler stood behind her and saw the seven-year-old boy staring up at Cora with that same dazed, lifeless expression. It hadn't changed once since Tom Poulter had brought him out of the woods.

The sheriff turned and went down to the kitchen.

There he phoned for replacements, then turned the pancakes and bacon, and poured himself a cup of coffee. He was drinking it when Cora came down the back stairs and returned to the stove.

"Are his parents—?" she began.

"I don't know," Wheeler said, shaking his head, "We couldn't get near the house."

"But the boy—?"

"Tom Poulter found him outside."

"Outside."

"We don't know how he got out," he said, "All we know's he was there."

His wife grew silent. She slid pancakes on a dish and put the dish in front of him. She put her hand on his shoulder.

"You look tired," she said, "Can you go to bed?"

"Later," he said.

She nodded, then, patting his shoulder, turned away. "The bacon will be done directly," she said.

He grunted. Then, as he poured maple syrup over the stack of cakes, he said, "I expect they are dead, Cora. It's an awful fire; still going when I left. Nothing we could do about it."

"That poor boy," she said.

She stood by the stove watching her husband eat wearily.

"I tried to get him to talk," she said, shaking her head, "but he never said a word."

"Never said a word to us either," he told her, "Just stared."

He looked at the table, chewing thoughtfully.

"Like he didn't even know how to talk," he said.

A little after ten that morning the waterfall came—a waterfall of rain—and the burning house sputtered and hissed into charred, smoke-fogged ruins.

Red-eyed and exhausted, Sheriff Wheeler sat motionless in the truck cab until the deluge had slackened. Then, with a chest-deep groan, he pushed open the door and slid to the ground. There, he raised the collar of his slicker and pulled down the wide-brimmed Stetson more tightly on his skull. He walked around to the back of the covered truck.

"Come on," he said, his voice hoarsely dry. He trudged through the clinging mud toward the house.

The front door still stood. Wheeler and the other men bypassed it and clambered over the collapsed living-room wall. The sheriff felt thin waves of heat from the still glowing timbers and the throat-clogging reek of wet, smoldering rugs and upholstery turned his edgy stomach.

He stepped across some half-burned books on the floor and the roasted bindings crackled beneath his tread. He kept moving, into the hall, breathing through gritted teeth, rain spattering off his shoulders and back. I hope they got out, he thought, I hope to God they got out.

They hadn't. They were still in their bed, no longer human, blackened to a hideous, joint-twisted crisp. Sheriff Wheeler's face was taut and pale as he looked down at them.

One of the men prodded a wet twig at something on the mattress.

"Pipe," Wheeler heard him say above the drum of rain, "Must have fell asleep smokin'."

"Get some blankets," Wheeler told them, "Put them in the back of the truck."

Two of the men turned away without a word and Wheeler heard them clump away over the rubble.

He was unable to take his eyes off Professor Holger Nielsen and his wife Fanny, scorched into grotesque mockeries of the handsome couple he remembered—the tall, big-framed Holger, calmly imperious; the slender, auburn-haired Fanny, her face a soft, rose-cheeked—

Abruptly, the sheriff turned and stumbled from the

room, almost tripping over a fallen beam.

The boy—what would happen to the boy now? That day was the first time Paal had ever left this house in his life. His parents were the fulcrum of his world; Wheeler knew that much. No wonder there had been that look of shocked incomprehension on Paal's face.

Yet how did he know his mother and father were dead?

As the sheriff crossed the livingroom, he saw one of the men looking at a partially charred book.

"Look at this," the man said, holding it out.

Wheeler glanced at it, his eyes catching the title: *The Unknown Mind.*

He turned away tensely. "Put it down!" he snapped, quitting the house with long, anxious strides. The memory of how the Nielsens looked went with him; and something else. A question.

How did Paal get out of the house?

Paal woke up.

For a long moment he stared up at the formless shadows that danced and fluttered across the ceiling. It was raining out. The wind was rustling tree boughs outside the window, causing shadow movements in this strange room. Paal lay motionless in the warm center of the bed, air crisp in his lungs, cold against his pale cheeks.

Where were they? Paal closed his eyes and tried to sense their presence. They weren't in the house. Where then? Where were his mother and father?

Hands of my mother. Paal washed his mind clean of all but the trigger symbol. They rested on the ebony velvet of his concentration—pale, lovely hands, soft to touch and be touched by, the mechanism that could raise his mind to the needed level of clarity.

In his own home it would be unnecessary. His own home was filled with the sense of them. Each object touched by them possessed a power to bring their minds close. The very air seemed charged with their consciousness, filled with a constancy of attention.

Not here. He needed to lift himself above the alien drag of here.

Therefore, I am convinced that each child is born with this instinctive ability. Words given to him by his father appearing again like a dew-jeweled spider web across the fingers of his mother's hands. He stripped it off. The hands were free again, stroking slowly at the darkness of his mental focus. His eyes were shut; a tracery of lines and ridges scarred his brow, his tightened jaw was bloodless. The level of awareness, like waters, rose.

His senses rose along, unbidden.

Sound revealed its woven maze—the rushing, thudding, drumming, dripping rain; the tangled knit of winds through air and tree and gabled cave; the crackling settle of the house; each whispering transience of process.

Sense of smell expanded to a cloud of brain-filling odors—wood and wool, damp brick and dust and sweet starched linens. Beneath his tensing fingers weave became apparent—coolness and warmth, the weight of covers, the delicate, skin-scarring press of rumpled sheet. In his mouth the taste of cold air, old house. Of sight, only the hands.

Silence; lack of response. He'd never had to wait so long for answers before. Usually, they flooded on him easily. His mother's hands grew clearer. They pulsed with life. Unknown, he climbed beyond. *This bottom level sets the stage for more important phenomena.* Words of his father. He'd never gone above that bottom level until now.

Up, up. Like cool hands drawing him to rarefied heights. Tendrils of acute consciousness rose toward the peak, searching desperately for a holding place. The hands began breaking into clouds. The clouds dispersed.

It seemed he floated toward the blackened tangle of his home, rain a glistening lace before his eyes. He saw the front door standing, waiting for his hand. The house drew closer. It was engulfed in licking mists. Closer, closer—

Paal, no.

His body shuddered on the bed. Ice frosted his brain. The house fled suddenly, bearing with itself a horrid image of two black figures lying on—

Paal jolted up, staring and rigid. Awareness maelstromed into its hiding place. One thing alone remained. He knew that they were gone. He knew that they had guided him, sleeping from the house.

Even as they burned.

That night they knew he couldn't speak.

There was no reason for it, they thought. His tongue was there, his throat looked healthy. Wheeler looked into his opened mouth and saw that. But Paal did not speak.

"So *that's* what it was," the sheriff said, shaking his head gravely. It was near eleven. Paal was asleep again.

"What's that, Harry?" asked Cora, brushing her dark blonde hair in front of the dressing table mirror.

"Those times when Miss Frank and I tried to get the Nielsens to start the boy in school." He hung his pants across the chair back. "The answer was always no. Now I see why."

She glanced up at his reflection. "There must be something wrong with him, Harry," she said.

"Well, we can have Doc Steiger look at him but I don't think so."

"But they were college people," she argued, "There was no earthly reason why they shouldn't teach him how to talk. Unless there was some reason he *couldn't.*"

Wheeler shook his head again.

"They were strange people, Cora," he said, "Hardly

spoke a word themselves. As if they were too good for talking—or something." He grunted disgustedly. "No wonder they didn't want to send that boy to school."

He sank down on the bed with a groan and shucked off boots and calf-high stockings. "What a day," he muttered.

"You didn't find anything at the house?"

"Nothing. No identification papers at all. The house is burned to a cinder. Nothing but a pile of books and they don't lead us anywhere."

"Isn't there any way?"

"The Nielsens never had a charge account in town. And they weren't even citizens so the professor wasn't registered for the draft."

"Oh." Cora looked a moment at her face reflected in the oval mirror. Then her gaze lowered to the photograph on the dressing table—David as he was when he was nine. The Nielsen boy looked a great deal like David, she thought. Same height and build. Maybe David's hair had been a trifle darker but—

"What's to be done with him?" she asked.

"Couldn't say, Cora," he answered, "We have to wait till the end of the month, I guess. Tom Poulter says the Nielsens got three letters the end of every month. Come from Europe, he said. We'll just have to wait for them, then write back to the addresses on them. Maybe the boy has relations over there."

"Europe," she said, almost to herself, "That far away."

Her husband grunted, then pulled the covers back and sank down heavily on the mattress.

"Tired," he muttered.

He stared at the ceiling. "Come to bed," he said.

"In a little while."

She sat there brushing distractedly at her hair until the sound of his snoring broke the silence. Then, quietly, she rose and moved across the hall.

There was a river of moonlight across the bed. It

flowed over Paal's small, motionless hands. Cora stood in the shadows a long time looking at the hands. For a moment she thought it was David in his bed again.

It was the sound.

Like endless club strokes across his vivid mind, it pulsed and throbbed into him in an endless, garbled din. He sensed it was communication of a sort but it hurt his ears and chained awareness and locked incoming thoughts behind dense, impassable walls.

Sometimes, in an infrequent moment of silence he would sense a fissure in the walls and, for that fleeting moment, catch hold of fragments—like an animal snatching scraps of food before the trap jaws clash together.

But then the sound would start again, rising and falling in rhythmless beat, jarring and grating, rubbing at the live, glistening surface of comprehension until it was dry and aching and confused.

"Paal," she said.

A week had passed; another week would pass before the letters came.

"Paal, didn't they ever talk to you? Paal?"

Fists striking at delicate acuteness. Hands squeezing sensitivity from the vibrant ganglia of his mind.

"Paal, don't you know your name? Paal? *Paal.*"

There was nothing physically wrong with him. Doctor Steiger had made sure of it. There was no reason for him not to talk.

"We'll teach you, Paal. It's all right, darling. We'll teach you." Like knife strokes across the weave of consciousness. *"Paal. Paal."*

Paal. It was himself; he sensed that much. But it was different in the ears, a dead, depressive sound standing alone and drab, without the host of linked associations that existed in his mind. In thought, his name was more than letters. It was *him,* every facet of his person and its meaning to himself, his mother and his father, to his life. When they had summoned him or thought his name it had been more than just the small hard core which sound made of it. It had been everything interwoven in a flash of knowing, unhampered by sound.

"Paal, don't you understand? It's your name. Paal Nielsen. Don't you understand?"

Drumming, pounding at raw sensitivity. Paal. The sound kicking at him. *Paal. Paal.* Trying to dislodge his grip and fling him into the maw of sound.

"Paal. *Try,* Paal. Say it after me. Pa-al. *Pa-al."*

Twisting away, he would run from her in panic and she would follow him to where he cowered by the bed of her son.

Then, for long moments, there would be peace. She would hold him in her arms and, as if she understood, would not speak. There would be stillness and no pounding clash of sound against his mind. She would stroke his hair and kiss away sobless tears. He would lie against the warmth of her, his mind, like a timid animal, emerging from its hiding place again—to sense a flow of understanding from this woman. Feeling that needed no sound.

Love—wordless, unencumbered, and beautiful.

Sheriff Wheeler was just leaving the house that morning when the phone rang. He stood in the front hallway, waiting until Cora picked it up.

"Harry!" he heard her call. "Are you gone yet?"

He came back into the kitchen and took the receiver from her. "Wheeler," he said into it.

"Tom Poulter, Harry," the postmaster said, "Them letters is in."

"Be right there," Wheeler said and hung up.

"The letters?" his wife asked.

Wheeler nodded.

"*Oh,*" she murmured so that he barely heard her.

minutes later, Poulter slid the three letters across the counter. The sheriff picked them up.

"Switzerland," he read the postmarks, "Sweden, Germany."

"That's the lot," Poulter said, "Like always. On the thirtieth of the month."

"Can't open them, I suppose," Wheeler said.

"Y'know I'd say yes if I could, Harry," Poulter answered, "But law's law. You know that. I got t'send them back unopened. That's the law."

"All right." Wheeler took out his pen and copied down the return addresses in his pad. He pushed the letters back. "Thanks."

When he got home at four that afternoon, Cora was in the front room with Paal. There was a look of confused emotion on Paal's face—a desire to please coupled with a frightened need to flee the disconcertion of sound. He sat beside her on the couch looking as if he were about to cry.

"Oh, *Paal*," she said as Wheeler entered. She put her arms around the trembling boy. "There's nothing to be afraid of, darling."

She saw her husband.

"What did they *do* to him?" she asked, unhappily.

He shook his head. "Don't know," he said, "He should have been put in school though."

"We can't very well put him in school when he's like *this*," she said.

"We can't put him anywhere till we see what's what," Wheeler said, "I'll write to those people tonight."

In the silence, Paal felt a sudden burst of emotion in the woman and he looked up quickly at her stricken face.

Pain. He felt it pour from her like blood from a mortal wound.

And while they ate supper in an almost silence, Paal kept sensing tragic sadness in the woman. It seemed he heard sobbing in a distant place. As the silence continued he began to get momentary flashes of remembrance in her pain-opened mind. He saw the face of another boy. Only it swirled and faded and there was *his* face in her thoughts. The two faces, like contesting wraiths, lay and overlay upon each other as if fighting for the dominance of her mind.

All fleeing, locked abruptly behind black as she said, "You have to write to them, I suppose."

"You know I do, Cora," Wheeler said.

Silence. Pain again. And when she tucked him into bed, he looked at her with such soft, apparent pity on his face that she turned quickly from the bed and he could feel the waves of sorrow break across his mind until her footsteps could no longer be heard. And, even then, like the faint fluttering of bird wings in the night, he felt her pitiable despair moving in the house.

"What are you writing?" she asked.

Wheeler looked over from his desk as midnight chimed its seventh stroke in the hall. Cora came walking across the room and set the tray down at his elbow. The steamy fragrance of freshly brewed coffee filled his nostrils as he reached for the pot.

"Just telling them the situation," he said, "About the fire, the Nielsens dying. Asking them if they're related to the boy or know any of his relations over there."

"And what if his relations don't do any better than his parents?"

"Now, Cora," he said, pouring cream, "I thought we'd already discussed that. It's not our business."

She pressed pale lips together.

"A frightened child *is* my business," she said angrily, "Maybe you—"

She broke off as he looked up at her patiently, no argument in his expression.

"Well," she said, turning from him, "It's true."

"It's not our business Cora." He didn't see the tremor of her lips.

When Wheeler entered the post office twenty

"So he'll just go on not talking, I suppose! Being afraid of shadows!"

She whirled. "It's *criminal!*" she cried, love and anger bursting from her in a twisted mixture.

"It's got to be done, Cora." He said it quietly. "It's our duty."

"*Duty.*" She echoed it with an empty lifelessness in her voice.

She didn't sleep. The liquid flutter of Harry's snoring in her ears, she lay staring at the jump of shadows on the ceiling, a scene enacted in her mind.

A summer's afternoon; the back doorbell ringing. Men standing on the porch, John Carpenter among them, a blanket-covered stillness weighing down his arms, a blank look on his face. In the silence, a drip of water on the sunbaked boards—slowly, unsteadily, like the beats of a dying heart. *He was swimming in the lake, Miz Wheeler and—*

She shuddered on the bed as she had shuddered then—numbly, mutely. The hands beside her were a crumpled whiteness, twisted by remembered anguish. All these years waiting, waiting for a child to bring life into her house again.

At breakfast she was hollow-eyed and drawn. She moved about the kitchen with a willful tread, sliding eggs and pancakes on her husband's plate, pouring coffee, never speaking once.

Then he had kissed her goodbye and she was standing at the living-room window watching him trudge down the path to the car. Long after he'd gone, staring at the three envelopes he'd stuck into the side clip of the mailbox.

When Paal came downstairs he smiled at her. She kissed his cheek, then stood behind him, wordless and watching, while he drank his orange juice. The way he sat, the way he held his glass; it was so like—

While Paal ate his cereal she went out to the mailbox

and got the three letters, replacing them with three of her own—just in case her husband ever asked the mailman if he'd picked up three letters at their house that morning.

While Paal was eating his eggs, she went down into the cellar and threw the letters into the furnace. The one to Switzerland burned, then the ones to Germany and Sweden. She stirred them with a poker until the pieces broke and disappeared like black confetti in the flames.

Weeks passed; and, with every day, the service of his mind grew weaker.

"Paal, dear, don't you understand?" The patient, loving voice of the woman he needed but feared. "Won't you say it once for me? Just for me? *Paal?*"

He knew there was only love in her but sound would destroy him. It would chain his thoughts—like putting shackles on the wind.

"Would you like to go to school, Paal? Would you? *School?*"

Her face a mask of worried devotion.

"Try to talk, Paal. Just *try.*"

He fought it off with mounting fear. Silence would bring him scraps of meaning from her mind. Then sound returned and grossed each meaning with unwieldy flesh. Meanings joined with sounds. The links formed quickly, frighteningly. He struggled against them. Sounds could cover fragile, darting symbols with a hideous, restraining dough, dough that would be baked in ovens of articulation, then chopped into the stunted lengths of words.

Afraid of the woman, yet wanting to be near the warmth of her, protected by her arms. Like a pendulum he swung from dread to need and back to dread again.

And still the sounds kept shearing at his mind.

● ● ●

"We can't wait any longer to hear from them," Harry said, "He'll have to go to school, that's all."

"No," she said.

He put down his newspaper and looked across the livingroom at her. She kept her eyes on the movements of her knitting needles.

"What do you mean, no?" he asked, irritably. "Every time I mention school you mention no. Why *shouldn't* he go to school?"

The needles stopped and were lowered to her lap. Cora stared at them.

"I don't know," she said, "It's just that—" A sigh emptied from her. "I don't know," she said.

"He'll start on Monday," Harry said.

"But he's frightened," she said.

"Sure he's frightened. You'd be frightened too if you couldn't talk and everybody around you was talking. He needs education, that's all."

"But he's not *ignorant,* Harry. I—I swear he understands me sometimes. *Without* talking."

"How?"

"I don't know. But—well, the Nielsens weren't stupid people. They wouldn't just *refuse* to teach him."

"Well, whatever they taught him," Harry said, picking up his paper, "it sure doesn't show."

When they asked Miss Edna Frank over that afternoon to meet the boy she was determined to be impartial.

That Paal Nielsen had been reared in miserable fashion was beyond cavil, but the maiden teacher had decided not to allow the knowledge to affect her attitude. The boy needed understanding. The cruel mistreatment of his parents had to be undone and Miss Frank had elected herself to the office.

Striding with a resolute quickness down German Corners' main artery, she recalled that scene in the Nielsen house when she and Sheriff Wheeler had tried to persuade them to enter Paal in school.

And such a smugness in their faces, thought Miss

Frank, remembering. Such a polite disdain. *We do not wish our boy in school,* she heard Professor Nielsen's words again. Just like that, Miss Frank recalled. Arrogant as you please. *We do not wish—* Disgusting attitude.

Well, at least the boy was out of it now. That fire was probably the blessing of his life, she thought.

"We wrote to them four, five weeks ago," the sheriff explained, "and we haven't gotten an answer yet. We can't just let the boy go on the way he is. He needs schooling."

"He most certainly does," agreed Miss Frank, her pale features drawn into their usual sum of unyielding dogmatism. There was a wisp of mustache on her upper lip, her chin came almost to a point. On Halloween the children of German Corners watched the sky above her house.

"He's very shy," Cora said, sensing that harshness in the middle-aged teacher. "He'll be terribly frightened. He'll need a lot of understanding."

"He shall receive it," Miss Frank declared. "But let's see the boy."

Cora led Paal down the steps speaking to him softly. "Don't be afraid, darling. There's nothing to be afraid of."

Paal entered the room and looked into the eyes of Miss Edna Frank.

Only Cora felt the stiffening of his body—as though, instead of the gaunt virgin, he had looked into the petrifying gaze of the Medusa. Miss Frank and the sheriff did not catch the flare of iris in his bright, green eyes, the minute twitching at one corner of his mouth. None of them could sense the leap of panic in his mind.

Miss Frank sat smiling, holding out her hand.

"Come here, child," she said and, for a moment, the gates slammed shut and hid away the shimmering writhe.

"Come on, darling," Cora said, "Miss Frank is here

to help you." She led him forward, feeling beneath her fingers the shuddering of terror in him.

Silence again. And, in the moment of it, Paal felt as though he were walking into a century-sealed tomb. Dead winds gushed out upon him, creatures of frustration slithered on his heart, strange flying jealousies and hates rushed by—all obscured by clouds of twisted memory. It was the purgatory that his father had pictured to him once in telling him of myth and legend. This was no legend though.

Her touch was cool and dry. Dark wrenching terrors ran down her veins and poured into him. Inaudibly, the fragment of a scream tightened his throat. Their eyes met again and Paal saw that, for a second, the woman seemed to know that he was looking at her brain.

Then she spoke and he was free again, limp and staring.

"I think we'll get along just fine," she said.

Maelstrom!

He lurched back on his heels and fell against the sheriff's wife.

All the way across the grounds, it had been growing, growing—as if he were a geiger counter moving toward some fantastic pulsing strata of atomic force. Closer, yet closer, the delicate controls within him stirring, glowing, trembling, reacting with increasing violence to the nearness of power. Even though his sensitivity had been weakened by over three months of sound he felt this now, strongly. As though he walked into a center of vitality.

It was *the young*.

Then the door opened, the voices stopped, and all of it rushed through him like a vast, electric current—all wild and unharnessed. He clung to her, fingers rigid in her skirt, eyes widened, quick breaths falling from his parted lips. His gaze moved shakily across the rows of staring children faces and waves of distorted energies kept bounding out from them in a snarled, uncontrolled network.

Miss Frank scraped back her chair, stepped down from her six-inch eminence and started down the aisle toward them.

"Good morning," she said, crisply, "We're just about to start our classes for the day."

"I—do hope everything will be all right," Cora said. She glanced down, Paal was looking at the class through a welling haze of tears. "Oh, *Paal.*" She leaned over and ran her fingers through his blond hair, a worried look on her face. "Paal, don't be afraid, dear," she whispered.

He looked at her blankly.

"Darling, there's nothing to be—"

"Now just you leave him here," Miss Frank broke in, putting her hand on Paal's shoulder. She ignored the shudder that rippled through him. "He'll be right at home in no time. Mrs. Wheeler. But you've got to leave him by himself."

"Oh, but—" Cora started.

"No, believe me, it's the only way," Miss Frank insisted, "As long as you stay he'll be upset. Believe me. I've seen such things before."

At first he wouldn't let go of Cora but clung to her as the one familiar thing in this whirlpool of frightening newness. It was only when Miss Frank's hard, thin hands held him back that Cora backed off slowly, anxiously, closing the door and cutting off from Paal the sight of her soft pity.

He stood there trembling, incapable of uttering a single word to ask for help. Confused, his mind sent out tenuous shoots of communication but in the undisciplined tangle they were broken off and lost. He drew back quickly and tried, in vain, to cut himself off. All he could manage to do was let the torrent of needling thoughts continue unopposed until they had become a numbing, meaningless surge.

"Now, Paal," he heard Miss Frank's voice and looked up gingerly at her. The hand drew him from the door. *"Come along."*

He didn't understand the words but the brittle sound of them was clear enough, the flow of irrational animosity from her was unmistakable. He stumbled along at her side, threading a thin path of consciousness through the living undergrowth of young, untrained minds; the strange admixture of them with their retention of born sensitivity over-laid with the dulling coat of formal inculcation.

She brought him to the front of the room and stood there, his chest laboring for breath as if the feelings around him were hands pushing and constraining on his body.

"This is Paal Nielsen, class," Miss Frank announced, and sound drew a momentary blade across the stunted weave of thoughts. "We're going to have to be very patient with him. You see his mother and father never taught him how to talk."

She looked down at him as a prosecuting lawyer might gaze upon exhibit A.

"He can't understand a word of English," she said.

Silence a moment, writhing. Miss Frank tightened her grip on his shoulder.

"Well, we'll help him learn, won't we, class?"

Faint mutterings arose from them; one thin, piping, *"Yes,* Miss Frank."

"Now, Paal," she said. He didn't turn. She shook his shoulder. *"Paal,"* she said.

He looked at her.

"Can you say your name?" she asked. "Paal? Paal Nielsen? Go ahead. Say your name."

Her fingers drew in like talons.

"Say it. Paal. *Pa-al."*

He sobbed. Miss Frank released her hand.

"You'll learn," she said calmly.

It was not encouragement.

He sat in the middle of it like hooked bait in a current that swirled with devouring mouths, mouths from which endlessly came mind-deadening sounds.

"This is a boat. A boat sails on the water. The men who live on the boat are called sailors."

And, in the primer, the words about the boat printed under a picture of one.

Paal remembered a picture his father had shown him once. It had been a picture of a boat too; but his father had not spoken futile words about the boat. His father had created about the picture every sight and sound heir to it. Great blue rising swells of tide. Grey-green mountain waves, their white tops lashing. Storm winds whistling through the rigging of a bucking, surging, shuddering vessel. The quiet majesty of an ocean sunset, joining, with a scarlet seal, sea and sky.

"This is a farm. Men grow food on the farm. The men who grow food are called farmers."

Words. Empty, with no power to convey the moist, warm feel of earth. The sound of grain fields rustling in the wind like golden seas. The sight of sun setting on a red barn wall. The smell of soft lea winds carrying, from afar, the delicate clank of cowbells.

"This is a forest. A forest is made of trees."

No sense of presence in those black, dogmatic symbols whether sounded or looked upon. No sound of winds rushing like eternal rivers through the high green canopies. No smell of pine and birch, oak and sense of presence in those black, dogmatic symbols whether sounded or looked upon. No sound of winds rushing like eternal rivers through the high green canopies. No smell of pine and birch, oak and hemlock. No feel of treading on the century-thick carpet of leafy forest floors.

Words. Blunt, sawed-off lengths of hemmed-in meaning; incapable of evocation, of expansion. Black figures on white. This is a cat. This is a dog. Cat, dog. This is a man. This is a woman. Man, woman. Car.

Horse. Tree. Desk. Children. Each word a trap, stalking his mind. A snare set to enclose fluid and unbounded comprehension.

Every day she stood him on the platform.

"Paal," she would say, pointing at him, "Paal. Say it. Paal."

He couldn't. He stared at her, too intelligent not to make the connection, too much afraid to seek further.

"Paal." A bony finger prodding at his chest. "Paal. Paal. *Paal.*"

He fought it. He had to fight it. He blanked his gaze and saw nothing of the room around him, concentrating only on his mother's hands. He knew it was a battle. Like a jelling of sickness, he had felt each new encroachment on his sensitivity.

"You're not listening, Paal Nielsen!" Miss Frank would accuse, shaking him, "You're a stubborn, ungrateful boy. Don't you want to be like *other* children?"

Staring eyes; and her thin, never-to-be-kissed lips stirring, pressing in.

"Sit down," she'd say. He didn't move. She'd move him off the platform with rigid fingers.

"Sit *down,*" she'd say as if talking to a mulish puppy.

Every day.

She was awake in an instant; in another instant, on her feet and hurrying across the darkness of the room. Behind her, Harry slept with laboring breaths. She shut away the sound and let her hand slip off the door knob as she started across the hall.

"Darling."

He was standing by the window looking out. As she spoke, he whirled and, in the faint illumination of the night light, she could see the terror written on his face.

"Darling, come to bed." She led him there and tucked him in, then sat beside him, holding his thin cold hands.

"What is it, dear?"

He looked at her with wide, pained eyes.

"Oh—" She bent over and pressed her warm cheek to his. "What are you afraid of?"

In the dark silence it seemed as if a vision of the schoolroom and Miss Frank standing in it crossed her mind.

"Is it the school?" she asked, thinking it only an idea which had occurred to her.

The answer was in his face.

"But school is nothing to be afraid of, darling," she said, "You—"

She saw tears welling in his eyes, and abruptly she drew him up and held him tightly against herself. *Don't be afraid,* she thought. *Darling, please don't be afraid. I'm here and I love you just as much as they did. I love you even more—*

Paal drew back. He stared at her as if he didn't understand.

As the car pulled up in back of the house Werner saw a woman turn away from the kitchen window.

"If we'd only heard from you," said Wheeler, "but there was never a word. You can't blame us for adopting the boy. We did what we thought was best."

Werner nodded with short, distracted movements of his head.

"I understand," he said quietly, "We received no letters however."

They sat in the car in silence, Werner staring through the windshield, Wheeler looking at his hands.

Holger and Fanny *dead,* Werner was thinking. A horrible discovery to make. The boy exposed to the cruel blunderings of people who did not understand. That was, in a way, even more horrible.

Wheeler was thinking of those letters and of Cora. He should have written again. Still, those letters should have reached Europe. Was it possible they were all missent?

"Well," he said finally, "You'll—want to see the boy."

"Yes," said Werner.

The two men pushed open the car doors and got out. They walked across the back yard and up the wooden porch steps. Have you taught him how to speak?—Werner almost said but couldn't bring himself to ask. The concept of a boy like Paal exposed to the blunt, deadening forces of usual speech was something he felt uncomfortable thinking about.

"I'll get my wife," said Wheeler, "The living room's in there."

After the sheriff had gone up the back stairs, Werner walked slowly through the hall and into the front room. There he took off his raincoat and hat and dropped them over the back of a wooden chair. Upstairs he could hear the faint sound of voices—a man and a woman. The woman sounded upset.

When he heard footsteps, he turned from the window.

The sheriff's wife entered beside her husband. She was smiling politely, but Werner knew she wasn't happy to see him there.

"Please sit down," she said.

He waited until she was in a chair, then settled down on the couch.

"What is it you want?" asked Mrs. Wheeler.

"Did your husband tell you—?"

"He told me who you were," she interrupted, "but not why you want to see Paul."

"*Paul?*" asked Werner, surprised.

"We—" Her hands sought out each other nervously. "—we changed it to Paul. It—seemed more appropriate. For a Wheeler, I mean."

"I see." Werner nodded politely.

Silence.

"Well," Werner said then, "You wish to know why I

am here to see—the boy. I will explain as briefly as possible.

"Ten years ago, in Heidelburg, four married couples—the Elkenbergs, the Kalders, the Nielsens, and my wife and I—decided to try an experiment on our children—some not yet born. An experiment of the mind.

"We had accepted, you see, the proposition that ancient man, deprived of the dubious benefit of language, had been telepathic."

Cora started in her chair.

"Further," Werner went on, not noticing, "that the basic organic source of this ability is still functioning though no longer made use of—a sort of ethereal tonsil, a higher appendix—not used but neither useless.

"So we began our work, each searching for physiological facts while, at the same time, developing the ability of our children. Monthly correspondence was exchanged, a systematic methodology of training was arrived at slowly. Eventually, we planned to establish a colony with the grown children, a colony to be gradually consolidated until these abilities would become second nature to its members.

"Paal is one of these children."

Wheeler looked almost dazed.

"This is a *fact?*" he asked.

"A fact," said Werner.

Cora sat numbly in her chair staring at the tall German. She was thinking about the way Paal seemed to understand her without words. Thinking of his fear of the school and Miss Frank. Thinking of how many times she had woken up and gone to him even though he didn't make a sound.

"What?" she asked, looking up as Werner spoke.

"I say—may I see the boy now?"

"He's in school," she said, "He'll be home in—"

She stopped as a look of almost revulsion crossed Werner's face.

"School?" he asked.

"Paal Nielsen, stand."

The young boy slid from his seat and stood beside the desk. Miss Frank gestured to him once and, more like an old man than a boy, he trudged up to the platform and stood beside her as he always did.

"Straighten up," Miss Frank demanded, "Shoulders back."

The shoulders moved, the back grew flat.

"What's your name?" asked Miss Frank.

The boy pressed his lips together slightly. His swallowing made a dry, rattling noise.

"What is your name?"

Silence in the classroom except for the restive stirring of the young. Erratic currents of their thought deflected off him like random winds.

"Your name," she said.

He made no reply.

The virgin teacher looked at him and, in the moment that she did, through her mind ran memories of her childhood. Of her gaunt, mania-driven mother keeping her for hours at a time in the darkened front parlor, sitting at the great round table, her fingers arched over the smoothly worn ouija board—making her try to communicate with her dead father.

Memories of those terrible years were still with her—always with her. Her minor sensitivity being abused and twisted into knots until she hated every single thing about perception. Perception was an evil, full of suffering and anguish.

The boy must be freed of it.

"Class," she said, "I want you all to think of Paal's name." (This was his name no matter what Mrs. Wheeler chose to call him.) "Just think of it. Don't say it. Just think: Paal, Paal, Paal. When I count three. Do you understand?"

They stared at her, some nodding. *"Yes,* Miss Frank," piped up her only faithful.

"All right," she said, "One—two—*three."*

It flung into his mind like the blast of a hurricane, pounding and tearing at his hold on wordless sensitivity. He trembled on the platform, his mouth fallen ajar.

The blast grew stronger, all the power of the young directed into a single, irresistible force. Paal, *Paal, PAAL!!* it screamed into the tissues of his brain.

Until, at the very peak of it, when he thought his head would explode, it was all cut away by the voice of Miss Frank scalpeling into his mind.

"Say it! Paal!"

"Here he comes," said Cora. She turned from the window. "Before he gets here, I want to apologize for my rudeness."

"Not at all," said Werner, distractedly, "I understand perfectly. Naturally, you would think that I had come to take the boy away. As I have said, however, I have no legal powers over him—being no relation. I simply want to see him as the child of my two colleagues—whose shocking death I have only now learned of."

He saw the woman's throat move and picked out the leap of guilty panic in her mind. She had destroyed the letters her husband wrote. Werner knew it instantly but said nothing. He sensed that the husband also knew it; she would have enough trouble as it was.

They heard Paal's footsteps on the bottom step of the front porch.

"I *will* take him out of school," Cora said.

"Perhaps not," said Werner, looking toward the door. In spite of everything he felt his heartbeat quicken, felt the fingers of his left hand twitch in his lap. Without a word, he sent out the message. It was a greeting the four couples had decided on; a sort of password.

Telepathy, he thought, *is the communication of impressions of any kind from one mind to another independently of the recognized channels of sense.*

Werner sent it twice before the front door opened.

Paal stood there, motionless.

Werner saw recognition in his eyes, but, in the boy's mind, was only confused uncertainity. The misted vision of Werner's face crossed it. In his mind, all the people had existed—Werner, Elkenberg, Kalder, all their children. But now it was locked up and hard to capture. The face disappeared.

"Paul, this is Mister Werner," Cora said.

Werner did not speak. He sent the message out again—with such force that Paal could not possibly miss it. He saw a look of uncomprehending dismay creep across the boy's features, as if Paal suspected that something was happening yet could not imagine what.

The boy's face grew more confused. Cora's eyes moved concernedly from him to Werner and back again. Why didn't Werner speak? She started to say something, then remembered what the German had said.

"Say, what—?" Wheeler began until Cora waved her hand and stopped him.

Paal, think!—Werner thought desperately—*Where is your mind?*

Suddenly, there was a great, wracking sob in the boy's throat and chest. Werner shuddered.

"My name is Paal," the boy said.

The voice made Werner's flesh crawl. It was unfinished, like a puppet voice, thin, wavering, and brittle.

"My name is Paal.

He couldn't stop saying it. It was as if he were

whipping himself on, knowing what had happened and trying to suffer as much as possible with the knowledge.

"My name is Paal. My name is Paal." An endless, frightening babble; in it, a panic-stricken boy seeking out an unknown power which had been torn from him.

"My name is Paal." Even held tightly in Cora's arms, he said it. "My name is Paal." Angrily, pitiably, endlessly. *"My name is Paal. My name is Paal."*

Werner closed his eyes.

Lost.

Wheeler offered to take him back to the bus station, but Werner told him he'd rather walk. He said goodbye to the sheriff and asked him to relay his regrets to Mrs. Wheeler, who had taken the sobbing boy up to his room.

Now, in the begining fall of a fine, mistlike rain, Werner walked away from the house, from Paal.

It was not something easily judged, he was thinking. There was no right and wrong of it. Definitely, it was not a case of evil versus good. Mrs. Wheeler, the sheriff, the boy's teacher, the people of German Corners—they had, probably, all meant well. Understandably, they had been outraged at the idea of a seven-year-old boy's not having been taught to speak by his parents. Their actions were, in light of that, justifiable and good.

It was simply that, so often, evil could come of misguided good.

No, it was better left as it was. To take Paal back to Europe—back to the others—would be a mistake. He could if he wanted to; all of the couples had exchanged papers giving each other the right to take over rearing of the children should anything happen to the parents. But it would only confuse Paal further. He had been a trained sensitive, not a born one. Although, by the principle they all worked on, all children were born with the atavistic ability to telepath, it was so easy to lose, so difficult to recapture.

Werner shook his head. It was a pity. The boy was without his parents, without his talent, even without his name.

He had lost everything.

Well, perhaps, not everything.

As he walked, Werner sent his mind back to the house to discover them standing at the window of Paal's room, watching sunset cast its fiery light on German Corners. Paal was clinging to the sheriff's wife, his cheek pressed to her side. The final terror of losing his awareness had not faded but there was something else counterbalancing it. Something Cora Wheeler sensed yet did not fully realize.

Paal's parents had not loved him. Werner knew this. Caught up in the fascination of their work they had not had the time to love him as a child. Kind, yes, affectionate, always; still, they had regarded Paal as their experiment in flesh.

Which was why Cora Wheeler's love was, in part, as strange a thing to Paal as all the crushing horrors of speech. It would not remain so. For, in that moment when the last of his gift had fled, leaving his mind a naked rawness, she had been there with her love, to soothe away the pain. And always would be there.

"Did you find who you were looking for?" the grey-haired woman at the counter asked Werner as she served him coffee.

"Yes. Thank you," he said.

"Where was he?" asked the woman.

Werner smiled.

"At home," he said.

From Shadowed Places

DR. JENNINGS HOOKED in toward the curb, the tires of his Jaguar spewing out a froth of slush. Braking hard, he jerked the key loose with his left hand while his right clutched for the satchel at his side. In a moment, he was on the street, waiting for a breach in traffic.

His gaze leaped upward to the windows of Peter Lang's apartment. Was Patricia all right? She'd sounded awful on the phone—tremulous, near to panic. Jennings lowered his eyes and frowned uneasily at the line of passing cars. Then, as an opening appeared in the procession, he lunged forward.

The glass door swung pneumatically shut behind him as he strode across the lobby. *Father, hurry! Please! I don't know what to do with him!* Patricia's stricken voice reechoed in his mind. He stepped into the elevator and pressed the tenth-floor button. *I can't tell you on the phone! You've got to come!* Jennings stared ahead with sightless eyes, unconscious of the whispering closure of the doors.

Patricia's three-month engagement to Lang had certainly been a troubled one. Even so, he wouldn't feel justified in telling her to break it off. Lang could hardly be classified as one of the idle rich. True, he'd never had to face a job of work in his entire twenty-seven years. Still, he wasn't indolent or helpless. One of the world's ranking hunter-sportsmen, he handled himself and his chosen world with graceful authority. There was a readily mined vein of humor in him and a sense of basic justice despite his air of swagger. Most of all, he seemed to love Patricia very much.

Still, all this trouble—

Jennings twitched, blinking his eyes into focus. The elevator doors were open. Realizing that the tenth floor had been reached, he lurched into the corridor, shoe heels squeaking on the polished tile. Without thinking, he thrust the satchel underneath his arm and began pulling off his gloves. Before he'd reached the apartment, they were in his pocket and his coat had been unbuttoned.

A penciled note was tacked unevenly to the door. *Come in.* Jennings felt a tremor at the sight of Pat's misshapen scrawl. Bracing himself, he turned the knob and went inside.

He froze in unexpected shock. The living room was a shambles, chairs and tables overturned, lamps broken, a clutter of books hurled across the floor, and, scattered everywhere, a debris of splintered glasses, matches, cigarette butts. Dozens of liquor stains islanded the white carpeting. On the bar, an upset bottle trickled Scotch across the counter edge while, from the giant wall speakers, a steady rasping flooded the room. Jennings stared, aghast. *Peter must have gone insane.*

Thrusting his bag onto the hall table, he shed his hat and coat, then grabbed his bag again, and hastened down the steps into the living room. Crossing to the built-in high fidelity unit, he switched it off.

"*Father?*"

"Yes." Jennings heard his daughter sob with relief and hurried toward the bedroom.

They were on the floor beneath the picture window. Pat was on her knees embracing Peter who had drawn his naked body into a heap, arms pressed across his face. As Jennings knelt beside them, Patricia looked at him with terror-haunted eyes.

"He tried to jump," she said, "He tried to kill himself." Her voice was fitful, hoarse.

"All right." Jennings drew away the rigid quiver of her arms and tried to raise Lang's head. Peter gasped, recoiling from his touch, and bound himself again into a ball of limbs and torso. Jennings stared at his constricted form. Almost in horror, he watched the crawl of muscles in Peter's back and shoulders. Snakes seemed to writhe beneath the sun-darkened skin.

"How long has he been like this?" he asked.

"I don't know." Her face was a mask of anguish. "I don't know."

"Go in the living room and pour yourself a drink," her father ordered, "I'll take care of him."

"He tried to jump right through the window."

"Patricia."

She began to cry and Jennings turned away; tears were what she needed. Once again, he tried to uncurl the inflexible knot of Peter's body. Once again, the young man gasped and shrank away from him.

"Try to relax," said Jennings, "I want to get you on your bed."

"No!" said Peter, his voice a pain-thickened whisper.

"I can't help you, boy, unless—"

Jennings stopped, his face gone blank. In an instant, Lang's body had lost its rigidity. His legs were straightening out, his arms were slipping from their tense position at his face. A stridulous breath swelled out his lungs.

Peter raised his head.

The sight made Jennings gasp. If ever a face could be described as tortured, it was Lang's. Darkly bearded, bloodless, stark-eyed, it was the face of a man enduring inexplicable torment.

"What *is* it?" Jennings asked, appalled.

Peter grinned; it was the final, hideous touch that made the doctor shudder. "Hasn't Patty told you?" Peter answered.

"Told me what?"

Peter hissed, apparently amused. "I'm being hexed," he said, "Some scrawny—"

"Darling, *don't*," begged Pat.

"What are you talking about?" demanded Jennings.

"Drink?" asked Peter. "Darling?"

Patricia pushed unsteadily to her feet and started for the living room. Jennings helped Lang to his bed.

"What's this all about?" he asked.

Lang fell back heavily on his pillow. "What I said," he answered, "Hexed. Cursed. Witch doctor." He snickered feebly. "Bastard's killing me. Been three months now—almost since Patty and I met."

"Are you—?" Jennings started.

"Codeine ineffectual," said Lang, "Even morphine—got some. Nothing." He sucked in at the air. "No fever, no chills. No symptoms for the AMA. Just—someone killing me." He peered up through slitted eyes. "Funny?"

"Are you serious?"

Peter snorted. "Who the hell knows?" he said, "Maybe it's delirium tremens. God knows I've drunk enough today to—" The tangle of his dark hair rustled on the pillow as he looked toward the window. "Hell, it's night," he said. He turned back quickly. "Time?" he asked.

"After ten," said Jennings, "What about—?"

"Thursday, isn't it?" asked Lang.

Jennings stared at him.

"No, I see it isn't." Lang started coughing dryly. "Drink!" he called. As his gaze jumped toward the doorway, Jennings glanced across his shoulder. Patricia was back.

"It's all spilled," she said, her voice like that of a frightened child.

"All right, don't worry," muttered Lang, "Don't need it. I'll be dead soon anyway."

"Don't talk like that!"

"Honey, I'd be glad to die right now," said Peter, staring at the ceiling. His broad chest hitched unevenly as he breathed. "Sorry, darling, I don't mean it. Uh-oh, here we go again." He spoke so mildly that his seizure caught them by surprise.

Abruptly, he was floundering on the bed, his muscle-knotted legs kicking like pistons, his arms clamped down across the drumhide tautness of his face. A noise like the shrilling of a violin wavered in his throat, and Jennings saw saliva running from the corners of his mouth. Turning suddenly, the doctor lurched across the room for his bag.

Before he'd reached it, Peter's thrashing body had fallen from the bed. The young man reared up, screaming, on his face the wide-mouthed, slavering frenzy of an animal. Patricia tried to hold him back but, with a snarl, he shoved her brutally aside and staggered for the window.

Jennings met him with the hypodermic. For several moments, they were locked in reeling struggle, Peter's distended, teeth-bared face inches from the doctor's, his vein-corded hands scrabbling for Jennings' throat. He cried out hoarsely as the needle pierced his skin and, springing backward, lost his balance, fell. He tried to stand, his crazed eyes looking toward the window. Then the drug was in his blood and he was sitting with the flaccid posture of a rag doll. Torpor glazed his eyes. "Bastard's killing me," he muttered.

They laid him on the bed and covered up the sluggish twitching of his body.

"Killing me," said Lang, "Black bastard."

"Does he really be*lieve* this?" Jennings asked.

"Father, *look* at him," she answered.

"You believe it too?"

"*I* don't know." She shook her head impotently. "All I know is that I've seen him change from what he was to—*this*. He isn't sick, Father. There's nothing wrong with him." She shuddered. "Yet he's dying."

"Why didn't you call me sooner?"

"I couldn't," she said, "I was afraid to leave him for a second."

Jennings drew his fingers from the young man's fluttering pulse. "Has he been examined at all?"

She nodded tiredly. "Yes," she answered, "When it started getting worse, he went to see a specialist. He thought, perhaps his brain—" She shook her head. "There's nothing wrong with him."

"But why does he say he's being—?" Jennings found himself unable to speak the word.

"I don't know," she said, "Sometimes, he seems to believe it. Mostly he jokes about it."

"But on what grounds—?"

"Some incident on his last safari," said Patricia, "I don't really know what happened. Some—Zulu native threatened him; said he was a witch doctor and was going to—" Her voice broke into a wracking sob. "Oh, God, how can such a thing be true? How can it *happen?*"

"The point, I think, is whether Peter, actually, believes it's happening," said Jennings. He turned to Lang. "And, from the look of him—"

"Father, I've been wondering if—" Patricia swallowed. "If maybe Doctor Howell could help him."

Jennings stared at her a moment. Then he said, "You *do* believe it, don't you?"

"Father, *try to understand.*" There was a trembling undertone of panic in her voice, "You've only seen Peter now and then. I've watched it happening to him almost day by day. Something is destroying him! I don't know what it is, but I'll try anything to stop it. *Anything.*"

"All right." He pressed a reassuring hand against her back. "Go phone while I examine him."

After she'd gone into the living room—the telephone connected in the bedroom had been ripped from the wall—Jennings drew the covers down and looked at

Peter's bronzed and muscular body. It was trembling with minute vibrations—as if, within the chemical imprisoning of the drug, each separate nerve still pulsed and throbbed.

Jennings clenched his teeth in vague distress. Somewhere, at the core of his perception, where the rationale of science had yet to filter, he sensed that medical inquiry would be pointless. Still, he felt distaste for what Patricia might be setting up. It went against the grain of learned acceptance. It offended mentality.

It, also, frightened him.

What good's another doctor going to do?"

The drug's effect was almost gone now, Jennings saw. Ordinarily, it would have rendered Lang unconscious for six to eight hours. Now—in *forty minutes*—he was in the living room with them, lying on the sofa in his bathrobe, saying, "Patty, it's ridiculous.

"All right then, it's ridiculous!" she said, "What would you *like* for us to do—just stand around and watch you—?" She couldn't finish.

"Shhh." Lang stroked her hair with trembling fingers. "Patty, Patty. Hang on, darling. Maybe I can beat it."

"You're *going* to beat it." Patricia kissed his hand. "It's both of us, Peter. I won't go on without you."

"Don't *you* talk like that." Lang twisted on the sofa. "Oh, Christ, it's starting up again." He forced a smile. "No, I'm all right," he told her, "Just—crawly, sort of." His smile flared into a sudden grimace of pain. "So this Doctor Howell is going to solve my problem, is he? How?"

Jennings saw Patricia bite her lip. "It's a—*her*, darling," she told Lang.

"Great," he said. He twitched convulsively. "That's what we need. What is she, a chiropractor?"

"She's an anthropologist."

"*Dandy*. What's she going to do, explain the ethnic origins of superstition to me?" Lang spoke rapidly as if trying to outdistance pain with words.

"She's been to Africa," said Pat, "She—"

"So have I," said Peter, "Great place to visit. Just don't screw around with witch doctors." His laughter withered to a gasping cry. "Oh, God, you scrawny, black bastard, if I had you here!" His hands clawed out as if to throttle some invisible assailant.

"I beg your pardon—"

They turned in surprise. A young Negro woman was looking down at them from the entrance hall.

"There was a card on the door," she said.

"Of course; we'd forgotten." Jennings was on his feet now. He heard Patricia whispering to Lang, "I *meant* to tell you. Please don't be biased." Peter looked at her sharply, his expression even more surprised now. "*Biased?*" he said.

Jennings and his daughter moved across the room.

"Thank you for coming." Patricia pressed her cheek to Dr. Howell's.

"It's nice to see you, Pat," said Dr. Howell. She smiled across Patricia's shoulder at the doctor.

"Had you any trouble getting here?" he asked.

"No, no, the subway never fails me." Lurice Howell unbuttoned her coat and turned as Jennings reached to help her. Pat looked at the overnight bag that Lurice had set on the floor, then glanced at Peter.

Lang did not take his eyes from Lurice Howell as she approached him, flanked by Pat and Jennings.

"Peter, this is Dr. Howell," said Pat, "She and I went to Columbia together. She teaches anthropology at City College."

Lurice smiled. "Good evening," she said.

"Not so very," Peter answered. From the corners of his eyes Jennings saw the way Patricia stiffened.

Dr. Howell's expression did not alter. Her voice remained the same. "And who's the scrawny, black bastard you wish you had here?" she asked.

Peter's face went momentarily blank. Then, his teeth clenched against the pain, he answered, "What's that supposed to mean?"

"A question," said Lurice.

"If you're planning to conduct a seminar on race relations, skip it," muttered Lang, "I'm not in the mood."

"*Peter.*"

He looked at Pat through pain-filmed eyes. "What do you want?" he demanded, "You're already convinced I'm prejudiced, so—" He dropped his head back on the sofa arm and jammed his eyes shut. "Jesus, stick a *knife* in me," he rasped.

The straining smile had gone from Dr. Howell's lips. She glanced at Jennings gravely as he spoke. "I've examined him," he told her, "There's not a sign of physical impairment, not a hint of brain injury."

"How should there be?" she answered, quietly, "It's not disease. It's juju."

Jennings stared at her. "You—"

"*There* we go," said Peter, hoarsely, "Now we've got it." He was sitting up again, whitened fingers digging at the cushions. "That's the answer. *Juju.*"

"Do you doubt it?" asked Lurice.

"I *doubt* it."

"The way you doubt your prejudice?"

"Oh, Jesus. *God.*" Lang filled his lungs with a guttural, sucking noise. "I was hurting and I wanted something to hate so I picked on that lousy savage to—"

He fell back heavily. "The hell with it. Think what you like." He clamped a palsied hand across his eyes. "Just let me die. Oh, Jesus, Jesus God, sweet Jesus, *let me die.*" Suddenly, he looked at Jennings. "Another shot?" he begged.

"Peter, your heart can't—"

"*Damn* my heart!" Peter's head was rocking back and forth now. "*Half* strength then! You can't refuse a dying man!"

Pat jammed the edge of a shaking fist against her lips, trying not to cry.

"Please!" said Peter.

After the injection had taken effect, Lang slumped back, his face and neck soaked with perspiration. "Thanks," he gasped. His pale lips twitched into a smile as Patricia knelt beside him and began to dry his face with a towel. "Greetings, love," he muttered. She couldn't speak.

Peter's hooded eyes turned to Dr. Howell. "All right, I'm sorry, I apologize," he told her curtly. "I thank you for coming, but I don't believe it."

"Then why is it working?" asked Lurice.

"I don't even know what's happening!" snapped Lang.

"I think you do," said Dr. Howell, an urgency rising in her voice, "And *I* know, Mr. Lang. Juju is the most fearsome pagan sorcery in the world. Centuries of mass belief alone would be enough to give it terrifying power. It *has* that power, Mr. Lang. You know it does."

"And how do *you* know, Dr. Howell?" he countered.

"When I was twenty-two," she said, "I spent a year in a Zulu village doing field work for my PhD. While I was there, the *ngombo* took a fancy to me and taught me almost everything she knew."

"Ngombo?" asked Patricia.

"Witch doctor," said Peter, in disgust.

"I thought witch doctors were men," said Jennings.

"No, most of them are women," said Lurice, "Shrewd, observant women who work very hard at their profession."

"Frauds," said Peter.

Lurice smiled at him. "Yes," she said, "They are. Frauds. Parasites. Loafers. Scaremongers. Still—" Her smile grew hard. "—What do you suppose is making you feel as if a thousand spiders were crawling all over you?"

For the first time since he'd entered the apartment,

Jennings saw a look of fear on Peter's face. *"You know that?"* Peter asked her.

"I know everything you're going through," said Dr. Howell, "I've been through it myself."

"When?" demanded Lang. There was no derogation in his voice now.

"During that year," said Dr. Howell, "A witch doctor from a nearby village put a death curse on me. Kuringa saved me from it."

"Tell me," said Peter, breaking in on her. Jennings noticed that the young man's breath was quickening. It appalled him to realize that the second injection was already beginning to lose its effect.

"Tell you what?" said Lurice, "About the longnailed fingers scraping at your insides? About the feeling that you have to pull yourself into a ball in order to crush the snake uncoiling in your belly?"

Peter gaped at her.

"The feeling that your blood has turned to acid?" said Lurice, "That, if you move, you'll crumble because your bones have all been sucked hollow?"

Peter's lips began to shake.

"The feeling that your brain is being eaten by a pack of furry rats? That your eyes are just about to melt and dribble down your cheeks like jelly? That—?"

"That's enough." Lang's body seemed to jolt he shuddered so spasmodically.

"I only said these things to convince you that I know," said Lurice, "I remember my own pain as if I'd suffered it this morning instead of seven years ago. I can help you if you'll let me, Mr. Lang. Put aside your skepticism. You *do* believe it or it couldn't hurt you, don't you see that?"

"Darling, *please,*" said Patricia.

Peter looked at her. Then his gaze moved back to Dr. Howell.

"We mustn't wait much longer, Mr. Lang," she warned.

"All *right!*" He closed his eyes. "All right then, *try.* I sure as hell can't get any worse."

"Quickly," begged Patricia.

"Yes." Lurice Howell turned and walked across the room to get her overnight bag.

It was as she picked it up that Jennings saw the look cross her face—as if some formidable complication had just occurred to her. She glanced at them. "Pat," she said.

"Yes."

"Come here a moment."

Patricia pushed up hurriedly and moved to her side. Jennings watched them for a moment before his eyes shifted to Lang. The young man was starting to twitch again. It's *coming,* Jennings thought. *Juju is the most fearsome pagan sorcery in the world—*

"What?"

Jennings glanced at the women. Pat was staring at Dr. Howell in shock.

"I'm sorry," said Lurice, "I should have told you from the start, but there wasn't any opportunity."

Pat hesitated. "It has to be that way?" she asked.

"Yes. It does."

Patricia looked at Peter with a questioning apprehension in her eyes. Abruptly, then, she nodded. "All right," she said, "but *hurry.*"

Without another word, Lurice Howell went into the bedroom. Jennings watched his daughter as she looked intently at the door behind which the Negro woman had closeted herself. He could not fathom the meaning of her look. For now the fear in Pat's expression was of a different sort.

The bedroom door opened and Dr. Howell came out. Jennings, turning from the sofa, caught his breath. Lurice was naked to the waist and garbed below with a skirt composed of several colored handkerchiefs knotted together. Her legs and feet were bare. Jennings gaped at her. The blouse and skirt she'd worn had revealed nothing of her voluptuous breasts, the sinuous abundance of her hips. Suddenly conscious of his blatant observation, Jennings turned his eyes toward Pat. Her expression, as she stared at Dr. Howell, was unmistakable now.

Jennings looked back at Peter. Due to its masking of pain, the young man's face was more difficult to read.

"Please understand, I've never done this before," said Lurice, embarrassed by their staring silence.

"We understand," said Jennings, once more unable to take his eyes from her.

A bright red spot was painted on each of her tawny cheeks and, over her twisted, twine-held hair, she wore a helmet-like plume of feathers, each of a chestnut hue with a vivid white eye at the tip. Her breasts thrust out from a tangle of necklaces made of animals' teeth, skeins of brightly colored yarn, beads, and strips of snake skin. On her left arm—banded at the bicep with a strip of angora fleece—was slung a small shield of dappled oxhide.

The contrast between the bag and her outfit was marked enough. The effect of her appearance in the Manhattan duplex created a ripple of indefinable dread in Jennings as she moved toward them with a shy, almost childlike defiance—as if her shame were balanced by a knowledge of her physical wealth. Jennings was startled to see that her stomach was tattooed, hundreds of tiny welts forming a design of concentric circles around her navel.

"Kuringa insisted on it," said Lurice as if he'd asked, "It was her price for teaching me her secrets." She smiled fleetingly. "I managed to dissuade her from filing my teeth to a point."

Jennings sensed that she was talking to hide her embarrassment and he felt a surge of empathy for her as she set her bag down, opened it and started to remove its contents.

"The welts are raised by making small incisions in the flesh," she said, "and pressing into each incision a dab of paste." She put, on the coffee table, a vial of grumous liquid, a handful of small, polished bones. "The paste I had to make myself. I had to catch a land crab with my bare hands and tear off one of its claws. I had to tear the skin from a living frog and the jaw from a monkey." She put on the table a bundle of what looked like tiny lances. "The claws, the skin, and the jaw, together with some plant ingredients, I pounded into the paste."

Jennings looked surprised as she withdrew an LP record from the bag and set it on the turntable.

"When I say 'Now,' Doctor," she asked, "will you put on the needle arm?"

"Jennings nodded mutely, watching her with what was close to fascination. She seemed to know exactly what she was doing. Ignoring the slit-eyed stare of Lang, the uncertain surveillance of Patricia, Lurice set the various objects on the floor. As she squatted, Pat could not restrain a gasp. Underneath the skirt of handkerchiefs, Lurice's loins were uncovered.

"Well, I may not live," said Peter—his face was almost white now—"but it looks as if I'm going to have a fascinating death."

Lurice interrupted him. "If the three of you will sit in a circle," she said. The prim refinement of her voice coming from the lips of what seemed a pagan goddess struck Jennings forcibly as he moved to assist Lang.

The seizure came as Peter tried to stand. In an instant, he was in the throes of it, groveling on the floor, his body doubled, his knees and elbows thumping at the rug. Abruptly, he flopped over, forcing back his head, the muscles of his spine tensed so acutely that his back arched upward from the floor. Pale foam ribboned from the slash of his mouth, his staring eyes seemed frozen in their sockets.

"Lurice!" screamed Pat.

"There's nothing we can do until it passes," said Lurice. She stared at Lang with sickened eyes. Then, as his bathrobe came undone and he was thrashing naked on the rug, she turned away, her face tightening with a look that Jennings, glancing at her, saw, to his added disquietude, was a look of fear. Then he and Pat were bent across Lang's afflicted body, trying to hold him in check.

"*Let him go,*" said Lurice, "There's nothing you can do."

Patricia glared at her in frightened animosity. As Peter's body finally shuddered into immobility, she drew the edges of his robe together and refastened the sash.

"*Now.* Into the circle, quickly," said Lurice, clearly forcing herself against some inner dread. "No, he has to sit alone," she said, as Patricia braced herself beside him, supporting his back.

"He'll *fall,*" said Pat, an undercurrent of resentment in her voice.

"Patricia, if you want my help—!"

Uncertainly, her eyes drifting from Peter's pain-wasted features to the harried expression on Lurice's face, Patricia edged away and settled herself.

"Cross-legged, please," said Lurice, "Mr. Lang?"

Peter grunted, eyes half-closed.

"During the ceremony, I'll ask you for a token of payment. Some unimportant personal item will suffice."

Peter nodded. "All right; let's *go,*" he said, "I can't take much more."

Lurice's breasts rose, quivering, as she drew in breath. "No talking now," she murmured. Nervously, she sat across from Peter and bowed her head. Except for Lang's stentorian breathing, the room grew deathly still. Jennings could hear, faintly, in the distance, the sounds of traffic. It seemed impossible to adjust his mind to what was about to happen: an attempted ritual of jungle sorcery—in a New York City apartment.

He tried, in vain, to clear his mind of misgivings. He didn't believe in this. Yet here he sat, his crossed legs already beginning to cramp. Here sat Peter Lang, obviously close to death with not a symptom to explain it. Here sat his daughter, terrified, struggling mentally against that which she herself had initiated. And here, most bizarre of all, sat—not Dr. Howell, an intelligent professor of anthropology, a cultured, civilized woman—but a near-naked African witch doctor with her implements of barbarous magic.

There was a rattling noise. Jennings blinked his eyes and looked at Lurice. In her left hand, she was clutching the sheaf of what looked like miniature lances. With her right, she was picking up the cluster of tiny, polished bones. She shook them in her palm like dice and tossed them onto the rug, her gaze intent on their fall.

She stared at their pattern on the carpeting, then picked them up again. Across from her, Peter's breath was growing tortured. What if he suffered another attack? Jennings wondered. Would the ceremony have to be restarted?

He twitched as Lurice broke the silence.

"Why do you come here?" she asked. She looked at Peter coldly, almost glaring at him. "Why do you consult me? Is it because you have no success with women?"

"What?" Peter stared at her bewilderedly.

"Is someone in your house sick? Is that why you come to me?" asked Lurice, her voice imperious. Jennings realized abruptly that she was—completely now—a witch doctor questioning her male client, arrogantly contemptuous of his inferior status.

"Are *you* sick?" She almost spat the words, her shoulders jerking back so that her breasts hitched upward. Jennings glanced involuntarily at his daughter. Pat was sitting like a statue, cheeks pale, lips a narrow, bloodless line.

"Speak up, man!" ordered Lurice—ordered the scowling *ngombo*.

"Yes! I'm sick!" Peter's chest lurched with breath. "I'm *sick*."

"Then speak of it," said Lurice, "Tell me how this sickness came upon you."

Either Peter was in such pain now that any notion of resistance was destroyed—or else he had been captured by the fascination of Lurice's presence. Probably it was a combination of the two, thought Jennings as he watched Lang begin to speak, his voice compelled, his eyes held by Lurice's burning stare.

"One night, this man came sneaking into camp," he said, "He tried to steal some food. When I chased him, he got furious and threatened me. He said he'd kill me." Jennings wondered if Lurice had hypnotized Peter, the young man's voice was so mechanical.

"And he carried, in a sack at his side—" Lurice's voice seemed to prompt like a hypnotist's.

"He carried a doll," said Peter. His throat contracted as he swallowed. "It spoke to me," he said.

"The fetish spoke to you," said Lurice, "What did the fetish say?"

"It said that I would die. It said that, when the moon was like a bow, I would die."

Abruptly, Peter shivered and closed his eyes. Lurice threw down the bones again and stared at them. Abruptly, she flung down the tiny lances.

"It is not Mbwiri nor Hebiezo," she said, "It is not Atando nor Fuofuo nor Sovi. It is not Kundi or Sogbla. It is not a demon of the forest that devours you. It is an evil spirit that belongs to a *ngombo* who has been offended. The *ngombo* has brought evil to your house. The evil spirit of the *ngombo* has fastened itself upon you in revenge for your offense against its master. Do you understand?"

Peter was barely able to speak. He nodded jerkily. "Yes."

"Say—*Yes, I understand.*"

"Yes." He shuddered. "Yes. I understand."

"You will pay me now," she told him.

Peter stared at her for several moments before lowering his eyes. His twitching fingers reached into the pockets of his robe and came out empty. Suddenly, he gasped, his shoulders hitching forward as a spasm of pain rushed through him. He reached into his pockets a second time as if he weren't sure that they were empty. Then, frantically, he wrenched the ring from the third finger of his left hand and held it out. Jennings' gaze darted to his daughter. Her face was like stone as she watched Peter handing over the ring she'd given him.

"*Now,*" said Lurice.

Jennings pushed to his feet and, stumbling because of the numbness in his legs, he moved to the turntable and lowered the needle arm in place. Before he'd settled back into the circle, the record started playing.

In a moment, the room was filled with drumbeats, with a chanting of voices and a slow, uneven clapping of hands. His gaze intent on Lurice, Jennings had the impression that everything was fading at the edges of his vision, that Lurice, alone, was visible, standing in a dimly nebulous light.

She had left her oxhide shield on the floor and was holding the bottle in her hand. As Jennings watched, she pulled the stopper loose and drank the contents with a single swallow. Vaguely, through the daze of fascination that gripped his mind, Jennings wondered what it was she'd drunk.

The bottle thudded on the floor.

Lurice began to dance.

She started languidly. Only her arms and shoulders moved at first, their restless sinuating timed to the cadence of the drumbeats. Jennings stared at her, imagining that his heart had altered its rhythm to that of the drums. He watched the writhing of her shoulders, the serpentine gestures she was making with her arms and hands. He heard the rustling of her necklaces. Time and place were gone for him. He might have been sitting in a jungle glade, watching the somnolent twisting of her dance.

"Clap hands," said the *ngombo*.

Without hesitation, Jennings started clapping in time with the drums. He glanced at Patricia. She was doing the same, her eyes still fixed on Lurice. Only Peter sat motionless. looking straight ahead, the muscles of his jaw quivering as he ground his teeth together. For a fleeting moment, Jennings was a doctor once again, looking at his patient in concern. Then, turning back, he was redrawn into the mindless captivation of Lurice's dance.

The drumbeats were accelerating now, becoming louder. Lurice began to move within the circle, turning slowly, arms and shoulders still in undulant motion. No matter where she moved, her eyes remained on Peter, and Jennings realized that her gesturing was exclusively for Lang—drawing, gathering gestures as if she sought to lure him to her side.

Suddenly, she bent over, her breasts dropping heavily, then jerking upward as their muscles caught. She shook herself with feverish abandon, swinging her breasts from side to side and rattling her necklaces, her wild face hovering inches over Peter's. Jennings felt his stomach muscles pulling in as Lurice drew her talon-shaped fingers over Peter's cheeks, then straightened up and pivoted, her shoulders thrust back carelessly, her teeth bared in a grimace of savage zeal. In a moment, she had spun around to face her client again.

A second time she bent herself, this time stalking back and forth in front of Peter with a catlike gait, a rabid crooning in her throat. From the corners of his eyes, Jennings saw his daughter straining forward and he glanced at her. The expression on her face was terrible.

Suddenly, Patricia's lips flared back as in a soundless cry and Jennings looked back quickly at

Lurice. His breath choked off. Leaning over, she had clutched her breasts with digging fingers and was thrusting them at Peter's face. Peter stared at her, his body trembling. Crooning again, Lurice drew back. She lowered her hands and Jennings tightened as he saw that she was pulling at the skirt of handkerchiefs. In a moment, it had fluttered to the carpeting and she was back at Peter. It was then that Jennings knew exactly what she'd drunk.

"*No.*" Patricia's venom-thickened voice made him twist around, his heartbeat lurching. She was starting to her feet.

"*Pat!*" he whispered.

She looked at him and, for a moment, they were staring at each other. Then, with a violent shudder, she sank to the floor again and Jennings turned away from her.

Lurice was on her knees in front of Peter now, rocking back and forth and rubbing at her thighs with flattened hands. She couldn't seem to breathe. Her open mouth keep sucking at the air with wheezing noises. Jennings saw perspiration trickling down her cheeks; he saw it glistening on her back and shoulders. No, he thought. The word came automatically, the voicing of some alien dread that seemed to rise up, choking, in him. No. He watched Lurice's hands clutch upward at her breasts again, proferring them to Peter. *No.* The word was lurking terror in his mind. He kept on staring at Lurice, fearing what was going to happen, fascinated at its possibility. Drumbeats throbbed and billowed in his ears. His heartbeat pounded.

No!

Lurice's hands had clawed out suddenly and torn apart the edges of Lang's robe. Patricia's gasp was hoarse, astounded. Jennings only caught a glimpse of her distorted face before his gaze was drawn back to Lurice. Swallowed by the frenzied thundering of the drums, the howl of chanting voices, the explosive clapping, he felt as if his head were going numb, as if the room were tilting. In a dreamlike haze, he saw Lurice's hands begin to rub at Peter's flesh. He saw a look of nightmare on the young man's face as torment closed a vise around him—torment that was just as much carnality as agony. Lurice move closer to him. Closer. Now her writhing, sweat-laved body pendulated inches from his own, her hands caressing wantonly.

"Come into me." Her voice was bestial, gluttonous. "Come into me."

"Get away from him." Patricia's guttural warning tore Jennings from entrancement. Jerking around, he saw her reaching for Lurice—who, in that instant, clamped herself on Peter's body.

Jennings lunged at Pat, not understanding why he should restrain her, only sensing that he must. She twisted wildly in his grip, her hot breath spilling on his cheeks, her body in rage.

"Get away from him!" she screamed at Lurice, *"Get your hands away from him!"*

"Patricia!"

"Let me *go!*"

Lurice's scream of anguish paralyzed them. Stunned they watched her flinging back from Peter and collapsing on her back, her legs jerked in, arms flung across her face. Jennings felt a burst of horror in himself. His gaze leaped up to Peter's face. The look of pain had vanished from it. Only stunned bewilderment remained.

"What *is* it?" gasped Patricia.

Jennings' voice was hollow, awed. *"She's taken it away from him,"* he said.

"Oh, my God—" Aghast, Patricia watched her friend.

The feeling that you have to pull yourself into a ball in order to crush the snake uncoiling in your belly. The words assaulted Jennings' mind. He watched the rippling crawl of muscles underneath Lurice's flesh, the spastic twitching of her legs. Across the room, the record stopped and, in the sudden stillness, he could hear a shrill whine quavering in Lurice's throat. *The feeling that your blood has turned to acid, that, if you move, you'll crumble because your bones have all been sucked hollow.* Eyes haunted, Jennings watched her suffering Peter's agony. *The feeling that your brain is being eaten by a pack of furry rats, that your eyes are just about to melt and dribble down your cheeks like jelly.* Lurice's legs kicked out. She twisted onto her back and started rolling on her shoulders. Her legs jerked in until her feet were resting on the carpet. Convulsively, she reared her hips. Her stomach heaved with tortured breath, her swollen breasts lolled from side to side.

"*Peter!*"

Patricia's horrified whisper made Jennings' head snap up. Peter's eyes were glittering as he watched Lurice's thrashing body. He had started pushing to his knees, a look not human drawn across his features. Now his hands were reaching for Lurice. Jennings caught him by the shoulders, but Peter didn't seem to notice. He kept reaching for Lurice.

"*Peter.*"

Lang tried to shove him aside but Jennings tightened his grip. "*For God's sake*—Peter!"

The noise Lang uttered made Jennings' skin crawl. He clamped his fingers brutally in Peter's hair and jerked him around so that they faced each other.

"Use your mind, man!" Jennings ordered, "Your *mind!*"

Peter blinked. He stared at Jennings with the eyes of a newly awakened man. Jennings pulled his hands away and turned back quickly.

Lurice was lying motionless on her back, her dark eyes staring at the ceiling. With a gasp, Jennings leaned over and pressed a finger underneath her left breast.

Her heartbeat was nearly imperceptible. He looked at her eyes again. They had the glassy stare of a corpse. He gaped at them in disbelief. Suddenly, they closed and a protracted, body-wracking shudder passed through Lurice. Jennings watched her, open-mouthed, unable to move. No, he thought. It was impossible. She couldn't be—

"*Lurice!*" he cried.

She opened her eyes and looked at him. After several moments, her lips stirred feebly as she tried to smile.

"It's over now," she whispered.

The car moved along Seventh Avenue, its tires hissing on the slush. Across the seat from Jennings, Dr. Howell slumped, motionless, in her exhaustion. A shamed, remorseful Pat had bathed and dressed her, after which Jennings had helped her to his car. Just before they'd left the apartment, Peter had attempted to thank her, then, unable to find the words, had kissed her hand and turned away in silence.

Jennings glanced at her. "You know," he said, "if I hadn't actually seen what happened tonight, I wouldn't believe it for a moment. I'm still not sure that I do."

"It isn't easy to accept," she said.

Jennings drove in silence for a while before he spoke again. "Dr. Howell?"

"Yes?"

He hesitated. Then he asked, "Why did you do it?"

"If I hadn't," said Lurice, "your future son-in-law would have died before the night was over. You have no idea how close he came."

"Granting that," said Jennings, "what I mean is— why did you deliberately subject yourself to such— abasement?"

"There was no alternative," she answered, "Mr. Lang couldn't possibly have coped with what was happening to him. I could. It was as simple as that. Everything else was—unfortunate necessity."

"And something of a Pandora's box as well," he said.

"I know," she said, "I was afraid of it but there was nothing I could do."

"You told Patricia what was going to happen?"

"No," said Lurice, "I couldn't tell her everything. I tried to brace her for the shock of what was coming but, of course, I had to withhold some of it. Otherwise, she might have refused my help—and her fiancé would have died."

"It was an aphrodisiac in that bottle, wasn't it?"

"Yes," she answered, "I had to lose myself. If I hadn't, personal inhibitions would have kept me from doing what was necessary."

"What happened just before the end of it—" Jennings began.

"Mr. Lang's apparent lust for me?" said Lurice, "It was only a derangement of the moment. The sudden extraction of the pain left him, for a period of seconds, without conscious volition. Without, if you will, civilized restraint. It was an animal who wanted me, not a man. You saw that, when you ordered him to use his mind, the lust was controlled."

"But the animal was there," said Jennings, grimly.

"It's always there," she answered. "The trouble is that people forget it."

Minutes later, Jennings parked in front of Dr. Howell's apartment house and turned to her.

"I think we both know how much sickness you exposed—and cured tonight," he said.

"I hope so," said Lurice. "Not for myself but—" She smiled a little. *"Not for myself I make this prayer,"* she recited, "Are you familiar with that?"

"I'm afraid I'm not."

He listened quietly as Dr. Howell recited again. Then, as he started to get out of the car, she held him back. "Please don't," she said, "I'm fine now." Pushing open the door, she stood on the sidewalk. For several moments, they looked at each other. Then Jennings reached over and squeezed her hand.

"Good night, my dear," he said.

Lurice Howell returned his smile. "Good night, Doctor." She closed the door and turned away.

Jennings watched her walk across the sidewalk and enter her apartment house. Then, drawing his car into the street again, he made a U turn and started back toward Seventh Avenue. As he drove, he began remembering the Countee Cullen poem that Lurice had spoken for him.

> Not for myself I make this prayer.
> But for this race of mine
> That stretches forth from shadowed places
> Dark hands for bread and wine.

Jennings' fingers tightened on the wheel.

"Use your mind, man," he said, "Your *mind.*"

BERKLEY'S FINEST SCIENCE FICTION!

Robert A. Heinlein

* * * * * *

Robert Silverberg